Untouchable

A NOVEL

2022 ©, SHON

ALL RIGHTS RESERVED.

BY SHON

Disclaimer

This is a work of fiction. Unless otherwise indicated, all the names, characters, businesses, places, events and incidents in this book are either the product of the author's imagination or used in a fictitious manner. Any resemblance to actual persons, living or dead, or actual events is purely coincidental.

Content Warning

Topics of childhood abandonment, anxiety, disorganized attachment, cheating, and difficult parent relationships are all brought up in-depth throughout this novel. If these are sensitive areas for you, please consider reading something else in my catalog.

Hey, boo

Thank you picking up this book. I hope you'll enjoy Pierre and Talulla's messy love story. Before you dive in, please note that Talulla is actively healing throughout the book. She's not perfect and she *will* get on your nerves. If you don't like frustrating female main characters, then maybe this isn't the book for you.

Dedication

To anyone who needs permission to fall apart.

Table of Contents

Talulla's Prologue 1

Pierre's Prologue 4

1. Talulla 8
2. Pierre 14
3. Talulla 26
4. Pierre 34
5. Pierre 40
6. Talulla 48
7. Talulla 52
8. Pierre 59
9. Talulla 71
10. Pierre 78
11. Talulla 85
12. Pierre 90
13. Talulla 96
14. Talulla 104
15. Talulla 111
16. Pierre 115
17. Pierre 124
18. Talulla 132
19. Pierre 139

20. Talulla	146
21. Pierre	151
22. Talulla	159
23. Pierre	169
24. Talulla	174
25. Pierre	180
26. Talulla	187
27. Pierre	194
28. Talulla	203
29. Pierre	210
30. Pierre	216
31. Talulla	223
32. Talulla	231
33. Pierre	237
34. Talulla	244
Pierre's Epilogue	250
Talulla's Epilogue	255

Talulla's Prologue

5 years ago...

Today is my boyfriend's wedding day.

At least that's what the post I'm looking at on Instagram tells me.

It popped up on my timeline innocently enough, but the dagger it pushed through my heart is anything but harmless.

lucas.hannon_
First Free Will Baptist Church

Under his username and the geotag is a picture of my "boyfriend," his hands intertwined with who I'm guessing is Gabriella. She's in a beautiful white gown. Her radiating smile only serves to further twist the dagger in its new home in my chest.

There's no mistaking what's happening here. And if there was any shred of confusion, it's wiped away when I read the caption.

"Today is the first day of the rest of our lives. I'm so blessed you chose me, Gabby. Just like I did before God earlier today, I vow to spend the rest of my life loving you and honoring you in every way a man can. I can't wait to spend the rest of my days with you."

Like the masochist I am, I click on his picture to reveal the tag and push the username that takes me to his new bride's page.

There's a similar, but long-winded, post on her page. My eyes burn as I skim over the caption.

Vomit threatens to push past my esophagus and come tumbling out of my lips.

Lucas. *My Lucas.* Is married.

What the fuck?

He told me he was going on a fishing trip to the coast with his brothers.

Kind of failed to mention there would be a wedding. Let alone, *his wedding.*

My head is spinning as I try to make sense of what I've just seen and read.

My boyfriend—Excuse me, my *ex*-boyfriend is married.

And he didn't even have the sense to delete me on Instagram before he posted boasting about it.

Still shocked, I don't even have the capacity to cry right now.

All I feel is a numbness blanketing me. No longer fazed by the dagger in my heart, I drop my phone on my bed and fall against the pillows.

I don't know how long I lie there, but disbelief has replaced the numbness when I emerge from my bedroom.

The man I've been in a relationship with for the last four years is married. To someone other than me.

The man I rearranged my life for and stayed in my college town for is married.

And I found out on Instagram.

Pierre's Prologue

It's been four days since Talulla showed up on my doorstep unexpectedly, sobbing and clearly not in the right frame of mind to have just driven four hours to get to me.

But when she started talking, I got it. We always sought each other during major storms in our lives and this time was no different.

From the moment we met in the driveway that summer, we've been attached at the hip.

That was twenty years ago, but I remember it like it was yesterday. We were ten years old and Talulla had opened her gap-toothed mouth and told me her name meant "abundance" and "princess". I've been addicted to her charm ever since.

That addiction grew stronger over the years, but I've never said anything.

And now definitely ain't the time. Not while she's on my living room floor crying her heart out over some motherfucker who never deserved her in the first place.

Since she got here, she's barely slept, and food hasn't touched her lips. She hadn't even looked twice at the carrot cupcakes I had specifically delivered for her.

Instead she's spent most of her time glued to her phone, alternating between aggressively scrolling and crying hard as hell.

Seeing her like this has me fucked up. Especially since I know that bitch ass nigga has probably already hopped a flight for his honeymoon. Meaning I can't go beat his ass like I want to.

"Fuck this," I hear from the floor. The sound of her hoarse voice makes me look up from the invoice I'm filling out.

From my position on the couch, I watch her delete the "Instagram" app from her phone and then turn to me.

"Can I use your computer?" she asks, sniffling.

Without hesitation, I save my progress and hand over my laptop.

"You have to use the desktop version to delete your account," she supplies even though I didn't ask.

"You're deleting your IG?" I ask, confused.

"Yea, I don't need this shit," she replies, sniffing some more.

As soon as she finishes the process, she bursts into full out sobs again, her shoulders shaking as she places my computer on the coffee table.

I thought that would have made her feel better. Clearly, I don't know shit.

Sighing, I drop down beside her on the floor and grab the box of Kleenex resting on the table.

"Tally," I say, hoping my voice is soothing. I never have to do this shit. Tally is not someone who gets visibly upset often so I'm out of practice, unsure of just how to comfort her, but wanting to all the same.

I'd do anything to dam the tears running down her mahogany cheeks right now.

"Look at me, Tally," I request, my fingers brushing away her tears and cupping her face as my eyes run over the delicate features of her face.

She's fucking stunning.

Even with her eyes red and puffy and her nose running from too much crying.

She looks like art: divinely sculpted, and perfectly put together by God.

Tally hiccups as she tries to stop crying, but she meets my eyes.

"Hey," I whisper softly. "Cry as much as you need. I'm right here, princess. And I'm not going anywhere."

Her eyes well up again before spilling over onto her cheeks.

I reach up with the tissue this time and wipe them away.

"Take as long as you need," I say, dropping a kiss against her forehead. "I'm not going anywhere."

She doesn't say anything after that, but she does fall into my embrace and stay there for what feels like hours.

I rock us back and forth as a ton of emotions tug at my heart, solidifying what I already know. Everything I love and everything I want is wrapped up in the person I'm currently holding. There's no way around it.

One day when she's ready to hear it, I'll tell her.

1.
TALULLA

PRESENT DAY

I am a simple woman and I govern my love life by four very simple rules:

1. No feelings
2. No sleepovers
3. No phone calls or FaceTime unless we are confirming plans
4. No more than one meet-up a week.

If a man can follow those rules, then he's good in my book. Unfortunately, a lot of them see it as a challenge and inevitably get their feelings hurt when they realize I'm serious.

But the only reason I maintain a semblance of my sanity is because I bend these rules for no one.

Well, *almost* no one.

I mean, how fun can life really be if we don't break the rules every now and then?

However, my date for the night, Isaac, is not someone I go around breaking rules for. Not even close.

Isaac James.

On paper, he's literally perfect for me. He's sweet. He's intelligent. He's *safe*.

But ever since we met in April, I have been trying to determine if I actually like him.

Here it is, nearly the end of July and I still don't know.

He's handsome. Extremely so. With his full head of 4C curls, an immaculate beard and piercing gray eyes. Eyes that always look so intent behind his rimless glasses. He's built like a football player, easily towering over my five-foot-four frame.

Not only is he easy on the eyes, but he's brilliant. As one of the youngest professors at the private university in my hometown, he would definitely make anyone's parents proud if they brought him home.

Like I said, absolute perfection on paper.

Meanwhile, he hasn't even met my friends. Much less, my father.

I think you spoke too soon.

The voice in my head is mocking as I watch my childhood best friend walk towards me with a date on his arm.

She's gorgeous, I muse to myself just as they come to a stop in front of us.

"Talulla," he says in greeting, his eyes and words exclusively acknowledging me despite the hard-to-miss-man at my side.

"Pierre," I say and quickly turn to Isaac, grabbing his hand as I make quick introductions. "Isaac, this is Pierre my best friend. Pierre, Isaac. The literature professor I told you about," I offer warmly.

My smile is firmly intact until Pierre openly scowls at me, then Isaac.

My eyes narrow at him and he has sense enough to wipe the grimace off of his face long enough to introduce us to his date, Kayla.

While he's playing nice, I have time to take in his appearance. Pretty dapper for a museum date. They must have gone somewhere before this. Navy slacks encase his long, athletic legs and a tailored, black button-down is tucked into them. Black leather shoes, his favorite diamond rope chain tucked inside his shirt but peeking from the collar, and his Hublot round out the look.

The line around his hairline is fresh, letting me know he went to see his barber at some point today. His low-cut hair is swimming with shiny waves and the dark stubble around his jaw tells me he hasn't shaved in a few days.

Pierre cleans up *nice.*

This is my favorite look on him and I almost get distracted by how good he looks.

Almost.

Thankfully, Kayla speaks, breaking my daze.

"Wait, this is Talulla?" his date asks, peering up at him with that megawatt smile.

She has the beauty of a pageant queen and I have to admit she looks great on his arm. She's exactly the type of woman I could see him ending up with.

Gorgeous. Well put together. Has an actual career. A dental hygienist according to Pierre's introduction. That would explain the perfect smile.

But Pierre hardly looks moved by it. *Poor girl.*

"We had your wine at dinner," she continues, causing my brow to stretch toward my hairline.

So, he'd talked about me on his date.

"It was perfect with our steak," she gushes, holding onto Pierre's arm. An arm I know is taut and corded with muscles thanks to the hours of manual labor he does at work... I shake away the thought. Pierre and his muscles are none of my concern right now.

"Thank you," I smile back at her, accepting the compliment as graciously as possible considering Pierre is staring a hole the size of Mars into the side of my face.

I try to focus on the small talk Kayla offers but it's a difficult task as he blatantly ignores Isaac's attempts to engage him in conversation.

He's such a damn grouch.

"I didn't expect to run into you here," he says fixing me with a look now that I'm not avoiding his eyes.

The heat in his brown eyes goes straight to my soul and I try not to focus on my heartbeat accelerating in my chest.

"It's an art museum, Pierre. Seems like a normal place for me to be," I say, and the wheels start turning in my head.

Had he shown up here on purpose? Did I accidentally mention my plans to him earlier this week?

I don't have the chance to give it much thought as my attention is brought back to the conversation happening right before me.

Isaac is speaking to Kayla about an upcoming poetry event and Pierre is…pouting.

Not in the traditional sense of the word, but he needs to fix his face nonetheless. Especially because I know exactly what he's doing. Mentally compiling a list of all the ways that Isaac isn't *enough* for me.

Long story short, Pierre doesn't approve of *any* of the men I date. It's complicated and I don't have time to get into it right now, but it'd be nice if he at least got better at hiding his attitude.

If Isaac is a golden retriever, then Pierre is a Doberman Pinscher. Do with that information what you will.

Later, after enough small talk to make my head spin and one too many deadly glares from Pierre, I manage to untangle Isaac and I from the situation.

"That guy looked like he wanted to kill me." Isaac's gray eyes look troubled after the exchange, and his forehead is sporting a fierce wrinkle that's actually endearing.

Pierre has definitely ruffled his feathers. But I don't have time to dwell on my best friend's psychological warfare right now.

Instead, I shrug and paste on the sweetest smile I have to offer. I tug at the locs hovering over my neck and breathe out, "He's just grumpy. It has nothing to do with you."

Isaac doesn't look at all soothed by what I have to say, so I infuse my smile with even more warmth.

"Come on," I say, grabbing his forearm. The muscles flexing under my touch don't go unnoticed. "I want to see the second-floor exhibits before we leave."

2.
Pierre

The body squirming under my touch is my own personal paradise and hell. Wrapped in one infuriating, petite shell.

She gets on my last fucking nerve, but I'll still move heaven and earth just so she's happy. Or in this case, just so she'll come.

"This is what you wanted, right?" I taunt as something close to a sob pushes past her throat and breaks free.

"Pierre, oh my god…" her voice is tight and pleading. Just how I like it. Just how I *love* it.

This is as close as I'm ever gonna get to her begging me for anything. The closest she'll ever co having any control. So I have to savor this shit. Prolong every minute until she's creaming on my chin and damn near speaking in tongues.

Her legs quake as I curve my index and middle fingers inside her pussy to coax another orgasm out of her as my tongue continues to tease her sensitive flesh.

"Pierre, I'm gonna come again," she whines, her pretty foot finding my left shoulder and trying to use it as leverage to push away from my tongue's assault.

She's always running from me.

"Stop fucking running from me, princess," I growl into her wetness, eliciting a shiver from her as she continues to defy me.

Thankfully, my free arm is locked around her left thigh making her no match for my strength as I pull her back to me every time she creates so much as an inch of space between us.

My greedy tongue swirls around her clit, thoroughly French kissing every decimeter of the distended ball of nerves. I could stay here for days and worship her lips, her clit, her walls. If she let me.

But she would never let me.

It's against her rules.

She comes down from her third…or fourth orgasm, panting. Her hands find my head and she begins trying to pull me upward.

I know exactly what she wants.

She wants me to kiss her while I sink my dick deep into her, filling her up in a way that my fingers can't.

"Pierre, I need you inside of me right now."

Even though I expected the words, they still put a smile on my face.

Of course, I'm going to give her what she wants.

Eventually.

It's always sweeter when she begs for it. My form of payback for the endless torture she puts me through.

With one last kiss to her leaking core, I pull my head away and withdraw my fingers. Slowly, purposefully running my thumb against her swollen clit just to get a reaction.

Her legs jerk and a stifled gasp leaves her mouth.

"Ask nicely, princess," I coach looking up at her face. "Ask nicely and I'll give you anything you want."

She's pulled to the edge of my bed, legs dangling now that the spot between her thighs is no longer occupied by my head.

I rise to my feet and look down at her with a smirk. Her chest is heaving as she stares back with lust in her eyes. Lust and a dash of annoyance for not giving her what she wants right away.

She's so fucking beautiful it hurts.

My dick is harder than hard and begging to be released from my briefs. But not yet.

"Pierre," she groans, a petulant pout on those perfect lips.

"Ask nicely," I repeat.

With a roll of her big golden-brown eyes, she huffs and props herself up on her elbows to stare at me from under her thick lashes.

"Pierre," she says.

"Yes, princess?"

"Would you please…" she pauses and licks her lips for added effect. I chuckle at the sight even though my dick twitches in response. "Come over here and put me out of my misery?"

Stepping out of my shorts, I rejoin her at the bed. Without warning, I grab her by the waist lifting her against my body in one movement. My dick slides against her clit and the folds of her pussy, but I don't go in. Not yet.

Greedily, she grinds against the erection situated between us trying her best to lift her hips and land on the one piece of me she craves.

But again, I easily steer her body to my liking. Head buried in her neck, I inhale the familiar scent of her.

As always, she smells like cinnamon, vanilla, and honey. My teeth graze her neck, pulling a moan from her throat.

"Pierre… I'll do anything," she chokes out, her arms wrap around my neck, toying with the hairs at my nape.

Hearing her say that is all I need before I plunge into her with a ferocity that shocks neither of us but pulls a moan from the both of us. We are always like this. Desperate. Insatiable. Rough.

A snug warmth surrounds my shaft, welcoming me and soaking me in the wetness of her desire. My hands slip from her waist and dig into the softness of her ass, holding her against me.

She feels so damn good.

She feels like home.

Her legs lock around my waist as she grinds against the pressure inside of her, begging me to move without saying a word.

Wordlessly, I turn and place a knee on the bed, keeping our bodies connected as we go from upright to horizontal.

The eyes that look up at me almost make me come on the spot. She has no right to be this damn fine. Everything I love is right there in those eyes.

Which is exactly why I chose this position. I want to see every emotion that passes over her face while I fuck the shit out of her.

Finally, I withdraw and look down at the point of connection. The slickness covering my dick is the best thing I've seen all day.

"Kiss me," she pleads as I fill her up again. My lips find hers without hesitation.

"Whatever you want, princess."

"Why'd you have to be so rude to my date?"

Of course, she's asking me this as I'm kneeling before her, wiping the remnants of my cum from the inside of her thigh. I fold the warm towel in half and laugh openly as I continue cleaning her legs.

Spoiled fucking brat. Just lying there fully confident in the fact that I'm going to do this for her. Each and every time. She's not wrong, but still…

"You really asking me that right now?"

"His feelings were hurt when you kept calling him the wrong name," Talulla supplied. Like I gave a fuck.

I'd wanted to break his hands for touching her, so he was lucky all he got was a mispronounced name.

Rage is all I feel whenever I get a reminder that I'm not the *only* one.

She might insist on introducing me as her best friend, but we both know it goes much deeper than that.

Isaac was added to the rotation at some point in the spring and I'm still lost on *why*. I don't even think she's attracted to ol' dude. But Tally claims she keeps him around to feed her love of art and culture. She keeps that other nigga she's seeing around because she barely has to see his ass and he likes dropping bags on her. She might deny it, but I know it's right up her alley. Low commitment, high reward type shit.

Where do I fit in? That's a good ass question. One I don't have the answer to. All I know is that mentally I'm somewhere between best friends with benefits and insane. Insane for agreeing to the shit, knowing damn well I'm in love with her and all she can offer me is…well, *this*.

"You want some tea?" I ask, rising to my full height and purposefully ignoring her previous statement.

I turn to look at her once I reach the doorway and she's sitting up on the edge of the bed, watching me. With those big, pouty eyes that make me forget shit. Like the fact that I'm supposed to be annoyed with her.

It's not like I've ever mastered the art of staying mad at Talulla anyway. Can't say I've tried very hard either.

"Pierre, you know how I feel about that possessive shit." Her voice is clipped as she continues watching me from the sheets we just ruined.

That made me kiss my teeth. *Here we go…*

"Yea, unfortunately I know how you feel about a lot of things, princess. Doesn't mean I understand them."

"You don't have to understand something to respect it."

"How the hell am I supposed to respect anything when I'm in love with you?"

Her eyes soften at my words as she bites her bottom lip. Like clockwork, her hand finds a cluster of locs at the nape of her neck and starts twisting.

She hates confrontation. And I hate feeling this way. But here we are.

In her typical avoidant fashion, Tally stands to start getting dressed. The thin gold chains around her neck and the gold hoop in her nose somehow still shining in the dim lighting of the room.

I notice the string of beads she wears faithfully fall dangerously low around her waist. Much lower than they usually do.

An instant glare takes over my face.

"You're dropping weight?"

Tally doesn't look fazed by my observation. Pulling her shirt over her head, she says, "I've just been skating more these days. You know how it is when I'm in the mood to be more active. I'll gain it back during the fall and winter when it's too cold to be outside. Or when I'm feeling lazy again. Whichever comes first," she laughs with a shrug.

Her explanation pushes away my concern. For now.

"Meet me in the kitchen when you're done in here," I say disappearing down the hall.

♥

Seated at the island in my kitchen, Tally smiles down at the cup of tea I just handed her. It had plenty of time to cool while she was in the shower.

"You know me so well," she comments, noticing the jar of honey and the sliced lemon on my countertop.

"Something like that," I remark, taking the barstool beside her. There was no need to fill in that I knew everything about her, even the parts of herself she tried to hide.

"I'm so tired." She yawns, stretching her body. "I don't want to drive home."

"So don't," I answer easily, an open invitation to spend the night with me. But I already know what her reply will be.

Her locs brush her shoulders as she shakes her head back and forth. "You know that's against the rules, Lancaster."

Tally and her fucking rules.

I don't know what's worse. Her roster. Or her damn rules.

Silence blankets the kitchen as she sips her tea. I know our time is almost up and I'm dreading it. I fucking hate this. But I love her. None of it makes any damn sense.

"Tell me more about Kayla," she prompts, brining an instant frown to my face.

"Nothing to tell."

"Come on, Pierre. There's got to be *something*. She was basically hanging off of you like a second skin at the museum."

I shrug, dismissing the observation. I'd been so preoccupied with Talulla at the museum that I hadn't noticed.

Kayla is…nice. Don't get me wrong. She's definitely easy on the eyes and I know for a fact that she likes me. My mama set us up after meeting her at a recent teeth cleaning appointment.

Leave it to Gwendolyn Lancaster to still find a way to talk me up when she's getting her teeth scraped.

Anyway, like I said, Kayla is nice. Real nice. She's just not Tally. And I don't want waste anymore of her time than I already have. So I know for a fact that tonight was our first and last time seeing each other. I should have never taken the date to appease my mama in the first place.

I have enough complicated emotions for Tally without adding someone else to the mix.

"You know," Tally says, oblivious to my thoughts, "I could see you ending up with someone like her."

I don't think the frown from earlier has left my face.

"What do you mean 'someone like her?'"

She shrugs, taking a long sip of tea.

"You know…someone stable. Someone *nice*. She seemed really nice."

"Compared to who?" I ask, my brow lifting. "You?"

"Honestly? Yea."

"I just told you I'm in love with you. Something you've known for weeks now and you're trying to pawn me off on another woman. That's wild."

My voice is even, and I push out a laugh, but any trace of humor is lacking.

"Pierre," she sighs, clearly wanting to drop the subject. But *she* brought it up.

"Talulla."

"I have to go."

"Why do you do this, Tally? Why do you deflect when I express my feelings for you?" I don't get it. I always thought women wanted partners who communicate openly. But then there's Talulla. A fucking anomaly if I ever met one.

"Pierre, I don't want to have this conversation right now."

Right. She *never* wants to have this conversation. Because of that we exist in this hellish loop of mind-blowing orgasms and tense, unspoken words. Deep down I know it's because of rule number one, but I occasionally dabble in delusion and let myself believe that because of our history, she'll eventually see me differently.

That shit ain't looking too promising though.

"Walk me to the door?" she asks, sliding off the stool to put her mug in the sink.

At the door, she falls against my body hugging me as tight as her arms will allow. Instinctively, I return the embrace wrapping her in my arms. I squeeze tight. Tally is a sucker for affection and it's one thing she lets me supply without her rules getting in the way.

She pulls away and sends half a wink my way. "Try not to miss me too much."

"Call me as soon you get home."

Her eyes double in size. "How about a text?"

"Don't play with me." I watch her, my gaze unwavering until she silently agrees to my command with a nod.

"Whatever you say, Pierre." Her tone is flippant, but I know she's going to do it.

I follow her to her car and stand in the driveway as she slides into the driver's seat of her coupe. I don't go inside until she's backed out and disappeared down the street.

I pass by the kitchen on my way to the living room and flick off the light. Once I'm on the couch I pull on my favorite green durag as my TV loads the Netflix app.

As I scroll through the shows, Talulla consumes my mind. I need to figure out what to do about her. Because we can't keep doing what we're doing. As good as it feels to have a piece of her, one of these days I'm going to lose my mind. More than I already have.

Every time I think we've struck a balance between torture and *whatever we're doing* she finds a way to tip the scales in her favor and leave me craving more. More that she can't—*won't*—offer.

Every time I look in Tally's eyes, I see nothing but my future. I don't know what she sees when she looks in mine though.

The only thing on my mind as I finally press 'play' on a series is: What the hell am I going to do about Talulla?

3.
Talulla

I wake up with the sun shining *right* in my face the next morning.

Wincing from the brightness, I turn towards the opposite wall and stretch under the sheets. A soreness lingers in my limbs from the night before, triggering instant flashbacks of what happened with Pierre after the museum.

A delicious smile takes over my face.

That man knows what the hell he's doing in bed. And he does it *so* well.

The thought sends a tingle up my spine and a breathy chuckle catches in my throat.

Everything is fine until I remember the look on his face *after*.

When he said those words that make my skin itch.

It's not the first time the subject has come up, but it doesn't make it any inevitably circle back to it.

Pierre is my best friend. My best friend who I sometimes fuck.

And lately, it's been way more frequently than *sometimes*. It's like my body can't get enough of him.

Out of the three men in my life, he's the only one I \. A rule we mutually agreed on. And it's fine by me. Because I have never been fucked by anyone the way Pierre fucks me.

My *goodness*.

Pierre Lancaster…

We've known each other since we were kids and I've somehow made a hot ass mess of our relationship. I know it. He knows it. Yet, we keep dealing with each other in a way that's going to burn us one day.

Sooner or later, I'm going to have to face the reality of just how twisted it all is. But today is not that day.

Shaking the troublesome thought from my head, I get out of bed and stretch one more time.

"Mornin' cuties," I sing towards the wall of plants in my bedroom. My justification for sleeping with the curtains surrounding my bay windows wide open. Pierre hates this minor detail, but truth be told he'd fuss about anything given the chance.

I head to the bathroom to get ready for the day. There's lot on my agenda for the day and I can't get lost in thoughts of Pierre. Otherwise, I won't get anything done.

A few minutes later in the kitchen, I bite into my buttered toast and thumb through the file folder in front of me.

Today's the day, I think as my hand grazes the edges of each document during my mental inventory.

Copy of my driver's license. Check.

Copy of my local background check. Check.

Printed out references. Check.

Completed application with my availability. Check.

All the documents necessary to become a volunteer storyteller at the local children's library.

I don't know why I'm nervous.

It's just a volunteer gig but for some reason, I really want this. More than I've wanted to do anything in a while. I say that as someone who's actively avoided work most of my adult life.

Plain and simple, I don't like labor.

Even with the winery slash bed and breakfast my father "gifted" me on my twenty-fifth birthday. It took me about six months to hire the perfect staff and then I was out of there. I have no problem splitting my profits with a capable staff if it meant less stress for me.

That's how I like to live my life: stress free.

So, this is a big deal.

I want this to work.

I'll be thirty in a few months. I'm gonna assume that's the reason I'm suddenly searching for meaning in life.

Okay, that's a bit dramatic, I'll admit.

But it would be nice to have something that excites me and makes me feel needed. It's something I've never experienced before.

I finish the tea in my mug and groan inwardly at the realization that it's not nearly as good as the cup Pierre made for me last night. How is that even possible? He only has tea in his house because of me and still manages to make it better than me even though he's a dedicated coffee drinker.

The nerve.

I swear, I don't think there's anything that man *doesn't* do well.

There I go thinking about him again.

I twist my face in a frown and glance over at the clock on my stove.

9:30.

I've gotta go.

♥

I didn't expect the children's library to be a trigger for me, but here I am: on the verge of panic and tears as I take it all in.

The warm, calming hues painted onto the walls, the quiet reading corners, and most importantly the *moms*. All here with their children.

Some smiling warmly at their offspring as they read together. Some clearly worn out as their kids run circles around them looking for a book. Some simply sitting in the too-small chairs as they wait for their kids to eventually circle back.

But there's one thing they all have in common. They're *here*. Present. Willingly or grudgingly, they're still here. Even though there's probably a mountain of other tasks they could be tackling at the moment.

My mother used to take me to the city library every week without fail when I was a kid. I'd read for hours on one of the droopy beanbag chairs as she sat in some far-off corner reading one of her many fashion magazines.

It used to be the highlight of my weekend.

I'd return the books I borrowed the previous week and then spend hours sifting through the stacks for the new ones I'd take home with me that week. My biggest worry then had been fitting all of the books into my favorite "book" bag. As an only child it was also the place where a lot of my social interactions with other kids took place.

Simpler times indeed. Until it had come to a halt.

Until Miriam woke up one morning and decided she'd had enough. That she didn't want to be a mom anymore.

Bile rises in my esophagus and my chest tightens at the thought.

Miriam was my mom. *Is* my mom. I suppose she's still alive. Not that it really matters. In my head, she died the day she abandoned me and my dad.

We didn't deserve tha—

"Ms. Evans, is everything alright?"

There's a hand at my shoulder and I know right away it's Birdie asking me the question.

The same Birdie I turned in my application to thirty minutes ago. The children's librarian that I need to impress if I'm going to land this gig. Volunteer or otherwise, this is important.

Snapping out of my head and back into the present moment, I give a jerky nod.

"Of course. Everything's fine," I lie without missing a beat, a smile brightening my face right on cue. The art of deception comes easily to me. Too easily.

Birdie looks skeptical. Her brow dips in concern as she moves her hand from my shoulder.

Leave it to me to space out in the vestibule. There's no telling how long I was standing there. But now I'm itching to get out of here. Away from Birdie's kind smile and concerned eyes.

"I'll see you around, Birdie. Thanks again for your time. I hope to hear from you all soon." It's all an echo of what I'd said earlier, but it is worth repeating.

Birdie nods as I begin to retreat. "We'll definitely be in touch, Ms. Evans. You have a good day."

♥

Outside, I can't pull enough air into my lungs to relieve the tightening at my chest. It all feels like too much as I try to ground myself back in reality, away from unwanted thoughts of the day my childhood was shattered, forever fragmented into segments of before and after I had a mother.

Blinking rapidly to offset the tears stinging my eyes, I look around searching for anything to dam the waterworks.

What can I see?

1. Palm trees spaced perfectly apart.

2. Cars crowded into the parking spaces near the entrance, leaving the rest of the lot fairly empty
3. The American flag

I draw in a deep breath and suddenly these things aren't blurry anymore.

Good job, Tally. Keep going.

My mother's clipped, cool voice is playing on a loop in my head, and I need to silence it.

What can I hear?

1. Squeaky car brakes
2. Rustling from the flag as the morning breeze hits it.
3. Kids laughing at the park across the street

Another deep breath and my heart no longer feels like it's gonna evacuate my chest.

I lick my lips. I flex my hand. And right on cue, my phone buzzes alerting me to a message.

It's Pierre.

Of course it is. He's calm personified and somehow knows exactly when to reach out to me.

My shoulders relax as I slide open the message and giggle at the meme about "plant moms" he's sent me.

As soon as I close his thread, a new notification from Jayce pops up. His message contains a picture as well, but it elicits a different type of thrill.

Matte black gift bags sit perched on his leather passenger seat and his text reads:

Miss you Lulu. When can I see you? I picked up some things for you while I was in Dubai.

My light mood slips firmly back in place as I type out my response and finally step off the sidewalk.

"I'm okay," I chant say to myself as I walk to my car. "I'm more than okay."

4.
Pierre

"Why you always bringing up old shit?" I grumble, cutting my eyes at Tally as she catches up with me.

"It happened yesterday!" Tally exclaims, her pretty eyes and slender neck rolling simultaneously. That shit is a skill honestly. And she looks good as hell doing it.

Even as she walks through the door of Gerrie's Diner with the other piece of our trio, Celeste, recounting how I *allegedly* ruined her date last night.

I pause by our go-to table near the back of the restaurant and pull out two chairs, waiting for my companions to drop down into them before I walk around to the other side.

"Damn, that's crazy," CeCe chimes in, with an amused but intrigued look on her face. "Tell me more."

"Why do you always support his crazy ass?" Tally grouses, shaking her head. "I ain't telling you shit. You're probably the reason he knew I was at the museum in the first place."

As soon as she says that my eyes fall to my phone. Because she's not wrong. But am I about to admit that shit out loud? Hell no.

"Y'all like to team up," Tally continues to mumble, and even though I'm not looking I know she's nodding like she's cracked the code. "Don't think I haven't noticed."

"I don't know what you're talking about, you know I can't stand Pierre's worrisome ass," CeCe deflects, bringing a smirk out of me.

CeCe is my ace for this exact reason. Ever since we met her in high school, she's always claimed I got on her nerves, but deep down I knew that shit was the furthest from the truth. She comes in clutch every time too.

Celeste is a wildcard in a lot of ways, but one thing she's never wavered on is that she wants to see me and Tally together. Eventually. To her way of thinking, we'll get it right *one of these days*.

I appreciate her optimism because most days my tank is on E when it comes to that.

Tally shifts the topic and I tune them out while we wait for the waitress to finally make her way to us. The service is anything but fast at this diner, but for some reason it's been our favorite spot since high school, and we keep showing up.

Half an hour later, we're finally eating and I notice Tally's gaze keep connecting with mine before she forces her eyes away. The last thing I want is for her to stop looking at me, but I am curious to know why her eyes seem to be pulled to me.

"Why you keep staring at me, princess?"

My question catches her off-guard. It's evident from the surprise that enters her eyes and the way she licks her lips.

Before Tally can formulate a response, CeCe jumps in.

"It's because you got on your hoochie daddy shorts today."

I glance down at my gray sweat shorts and burst out laughing. "Word, Tally?"

Tally's jaw drops as she swings her eyes from me to CeCe. "CeCe!"

CeCe takes her time finishing the last bite of her waffle before saying, "What? It's true. You been burning a hole in his shorts since he picked us from the shop earlier."

I throw my head back, still laughing as I try to remember if what she's saying is true. When I pulled up to Celeste's shop earlier all I had been able to focus on was how good Tally looked in the deep brown set that CeCe had her wearing for promo pics.

Whether Tally had been "staring a hole" in my shorts was lost on me. But the thought got a good laugh out of me and fed my ego at the same time. It was nice knowing that other people could pick up on her attraction to me and that it wasn't just in my head. Because sometimes it felt that way.

"I can't stand y'all," Tally says, shaking her head and refusing to look up from her French toast.

"You can't stand us, but you damn sure love us." CeCe bumped her shoulder with her own. "Especially me."

"Not when you're the one helping Pierre's rude ass pop up on my dates."

Here we go with that shit again…

One of these days she was going to learn I didn't give a fuck about her dates. Especially when she wouldn't entertain the thoughts of a real date with me. So, hell nah I wasn't letting up when it came to these other niggas. *Fuck that.*

I stare at Tally across the table. Really stare at her. The petulant set of her mouth and the frown trying—and failing—to form doesn't do anything but make me smirk more. This act is cute, but I knew she isn't really upset. If she was, she'd be silent and not sitting here talking about it.

Still, I can't give up the chance to tease her and test out whether she can get that frown to fully form.

"You weren't complaining when my tongue was in your—"

I see Tally's eyes widen, anticipating what I'm about to say next.

Before I can finish, all I hear is CeCe dry heaving dramatically followed by her voice shouting, "Check please!"

♥

Twin clipboards are in my hand as I drop down into a chair beside Tally in this cold ass waiting room.

"Why does every part of getting tested have to be uncomfortable? You want me to freeze in your waiting room and then stick swabs down my throat and up my vagina. Madness," Talulla muttered, leaning against my side.

Someone in a nearby chair hummed in agreement and all I could do was give a low chuckle. I love her grumpy ass. She's usually all sunshine and smiles, but not in this place. And I can't really blame her.

We agreed before ever starting our "arrangement" that we'd get tested together regularly. So, that's exactly what we've been doing. One year and four tests later, here we are. Which is crazy to think about it. A whole-ass year since I lost my rabbit ass mind and agreed to this shit knowing damn well casual sex with her would ruin me.

We complete our paperwork and get called back five minutes later. We get screened in separate rooms and when that's over, I find Tally waiting for her birth control consultation. It's the last thing we need to do before we leave.

I walk into the room fully intent to turn around in less than thirty seconds and return to that frigid ass waiting room.

"I'll be out there when you get done aight?"

I can't resist touching her whenever she looks up at me with those orbs speckled in gold. Her eyes are my weakness. Hell, everything about her is my weakness. I'm pushing her locs away from her face when she asks, "Stay with me?"

It never crosses my mind to deny her, but I am curious. I've never sat in on this part and since we aren't actually "together," it never occurred to me that she would even want me to.

Ten minutes later, I'm glad I stayed.

The doctor turns away from her computer and asks, "It's been six months since we started you on the progestin only pill. So how have things been since you started it? Any noticeable changes or complaints?"

Tally only shrugs, making me frown.

"Didn't you tell me it was fucking with your appetite and giving you headaches?"

She looks over at me with a raised brow, like she's surprised I'd remembered. Either that or she's shocked I'm saying something. But hell, if she wasn't going to advocate for herself I wasn't gonna sit here and watch it unfold.

"I thought that was normal with any birth control you take," Tally says, looking at the doctor expectantly for her take on it. "Is there really anything that can be done? Aside from not taking it?"

By now the doctor is nodding adamantly. "Great question. There are some side effects that we typically expect when your body is getting used to the new routine. But we don't want to normalize anything that's disrupting your daily norm."

I watch as Tally bites down on her lip before speaking. "So what are the other options?"

The doctor inclines her head at the question. "Well, there are a few non-hormonal options we can discuss…"

♥

5.
Pierre

"Dad's looking for you," my baby brother Marcus announces as he walks past me and towards the door I just came in through.

"For what?" I ask, turning my head as I keep walking inside of the building.

Marc shrugs, his full attention on his phone screen as he continues walking out the door. "I don't know," he tosses over his shoulder.

I shake my head at his lack of details and check my watch.

It's officially past closing time and I just got back from a job site to do some paperwork that can't wait 'til Monday.

Hopefully, whatever the old man wants to talk about isn't time consuming.

"What's up Pops?" I ask as my knuckles rap against his open office door.

He's sitting at his desk, deep in some paperwork but looks up to smile at me when I sit across from him in the visitor's chair.

"PJ!" he roars, his tone thunderous as usual. Pierre Lancaster Sr. is a lot of things, but a quiet man isn't one of them.

I lean back in my chair and wait for him to tell me why I was summoned.

"How'd the wrap up at the shopping plaza go?" he asks, closing the file folder in front of him.

Because my brothers were occupied with other aspects of the company, I was in charge of the final rollout for the grand opening of a new strip mall up the road. Despite some minor setbacks early on in the project, things had wrapped up nicely and I'm ready to celebrating that win this weekend.

I tell my dad as much and he looks happy with this update before folding his hands on top of the folder he'd been reading before I walked in.

"I need to talk to you about something, son." His voice is neutral, giving me no hints as to what this might be about.

My mind instantly pings to the two most extreme options.

He's retiring and this is how he plans to tell me that it's my turn to take over.

He's somehow hidden some money trouble from me and the landscaping business we own is going under.

Though I'm not the oldest, I am my father's eldest biological son. As my mom's second-born and my dad's firstborn, I became a "junior" on a technicality. My dad treats my oldest brother Josh just like his flesh and blood. But Josh has made it very clear that he only does this job for income and has no interest in taking on more responsibility in the future. So, naturally that would leave me.

I've gotten so deep into my thoughts that by the time my father speaks up again, I'm surprised by what falls from his lips.

"You know we've been looking for ways to expand into other areas for a while. We've been doing pretty consistent numbers here in Belle View and I think it's time we go a little broader."

Makes sense.

My dad scratches his peppery beard and says, "We just bought out a company up north and when the paperwork is done, I'll need someone to go up there and oversee the merging process. Get the workers acquainted with how we do things. So on and so forth."

"What are you saying, Dad?"

"I know how much you enjoy…uh," he pauses to gesture with his hands as he thinks of the right words. "*Managing* things."

I chuckle because I know this nigga wanted to call me a control freak. Not my fault I inherited my mom's perfectionist trait.

Talulla says it's because I'm a Virgo. Marcus says it 'cause I don't get enough pussy.

Regardless of the reason, this is how I've been for as long as I can remember.

"So what do you say?" my dad asks, watching me from across the desk.

I must have missed something because I don't remember him asking me a question.

"What do I say to what?" I ask for clarification.

"Going up there and getting things off the ground," he smiles and leans back with his hands behind his head. "Maybe a change of scenery, a change of pace is what you need."

I frown at that.

"What you mean by that?"

My dad exhales dramatically and sits forward again.

"Look son, we've all noticed how on edge you've been lately. Maybe a break away from…Belle View is what you need. To clear your head and all that good shit."

Of course, I know Belle View in this context is code for Talulla.

Not many people know about our…*thing*. But the ones who do don't get my attachment to her. Which is fine because I owe none of them an explanation.

But it's news to me that they think I'm on edge to the point that I need to relocate.

Fuck's sake.

My frustration with the situation has been getting to me lately. I just didn't know it was so *evident*.

I drag a hand down my beard and study my work boots as my mind starts racing.

Moving *would* take me out of this loop. Maybe I do need time away.

But am I really down to just leave? To give her the chance to get used to my absence. I've considered the possibility countless times. But is it what I want? For real?

"Listen, son," my dad says when my silence stretches on a little too long. "We don't have to make any decisions for another few weeks. But think about it. I know it sounds like a lot right now but sleep on it. Ultimately the choice is yours, I won't ship you off or give you an ultimatum," he clarifies.

"Aight."

"Sleep on it this weekend and get back to me."

I nod and excuse myself from the room, telling him that I have some paperwork to finish.

He stares at me long and hard but says no more as I leave and head towards my office with thoughts moving through my head at the speed of light.

What the hell am I going to do about Talulla?

The question from a few nights ago plays over and over. I didn't expect to receive an out so soon.

Now the only question is whether I'm going to take it.

A sane man would. But I've never claimed to be a sane man.

♥

My older brother Joshua is staring at me through narrowed eyes across the table from me.

His hulk-like frame looks comical folded into the booth while Marcus and I occupy the other side.

After a hectic week, the three of us decided to grab dinner and shoot the shit before going our separate ways to enjoy the weekend.

"So, Pops is trying to relocate your ass?" Josh questions, shoving the celery that came with his wings into his mouth.

I divide a glance between my two brothers as I take a slow pull from my first—and last—beer of the night.

Marcus is the youngest. Three years my junior, he is the outspoken and the most chill out of all three of us. We both stand at about the same height of six-two and love basketball, but that's about where our similarities end. He likes to do shit on the fly and let things fall in place as he goes, and I can't say I relate to that mentality.

Then there's Joshua. Standing at six-five, he's only one year older than me, but it feels like at least five. His quiet, serious personality has always made him seem more mature. Landscaper by day and bodybuilder by night, he got the nickname "Hulk" when we discovered just how much he loved putting on mass and then going on cuts to get ready for competitions. Even though he's quiet, that nigga can go from zero to a thousand in a matter of seconds so people usually leave his ass alone.

As the middle child, I've always felt like the neutral, levelheaded one. A middle ground for their contrasting personalities.

We all work for the family business but because they have interests outside of our inherited career path, I ended up with the most responsibility. Hence why I'm second in command and facing relocation right about now.

Placing my bottle back on the table, I nod slowly.

"Yea, he wants me to overlook the merging process."

"Shiiit," Marcus intones lowly. "That place makes Belle View look like New York City. I'd be bored as shit," he says, voicing a thought similar to one I had earlier today.

Not that I need to be entertained around the clock, but the option would be nice. After leaving my dad's office earlier, I looked up the town and his assessment is spot on. I'd probably be bored out of my mind if I decided to go.

Bored and going crazy because Talulla won't be around the corner…

But that's a different conversation.

"You going?" Josh asks, getting straight the point.

Shrugging, I tell him all I know so far, "He said I got time to think about it. Don't know who would go if I didn't, to be honest."

"Josh's brolic ass could go," Marcus jokes.

Josh only narrows his eyes in response.

"Or Lewis," Marcus says, mentioning our company's operations manager. "That shit is right up his alley."

Now *that's* a viable option, I think to myself. It makes the most sense *if* I end up choosing not to go.

"Plus, I know you not trying to leave Talulla behind," Marcus follows up, saying too much from the look on Josh's face.

"What about Tally?" he asks immediately, interest piqued.

Shooting a glare in my younger brother's direction, I shake my head. "Nothing."

"Yea, aight." Marcus finishes the whisky in his glass and looks at both of us. "One day we going to talk about how both you and Josh are in love with women who run circles around y'all's asses. Wouldn't let that shit happen to me though."

Instantly reminded of the episode of the Boondocks he just quoted, I'm amused instead of annoyed. I let off a low chuckle and look at Josh. If he was a shade lighter, that nigga would be blushing right now.

Brandy Hinton has had his nose wide open for the last year and he hasn't done shit about it.

Not that I can talk. But shit, at least Tally knows what's up when it comes to my feelings. Josh prefers to do his simping from afar. It's crazy to watch a man his size be so damn timid when it comes to women.

Clearly uninterested in furthering this conversation, Josh raises his arm to flag down the waiter.

"I'm getting out of here."

6.
TALULLA

Focus, Talulla.

It's a useless mantra as I gather my hair up into a high ponytail only to let the locs fall around my shoulders seconds later.

I'm supposed to be getting ready for a date. What am I doing instead? Daydreaming about that damn Pierre.

Trust me, I'm shaking my damn head too.

He's *all* I've been able to think about since we left the doctor's office two days ago.

I don't know what's been going on lately, but I can barely make it through a simple task without getting lost in a trance with him at the forefront of my mind.

Nothing he'd done was inherently groundbreaking. Nonetheless, I can't stop replaying the scene in my head.

Pierre in a doctor's office talking about birth control. Of all the things I could fixate on when it comes to that man, my heart—ahem, my brain *would* choose this one.

I swipe the lipstick across my lips, eyeing myself in the mirror as my thoughts continue to spiral out of control. It's a weird feeling, too. I'm not even turned on. *That*, I can deal with. But I do feel something. A whole lot of something that I told myself is off-limits when it comes to men. *Especially* him.

My ringing doorbell saves me from having to examine that unnamed emotion.

"Lulu, you look exquisite," Jayce compliments as soon as I open the door. He leans down briefly to brush a kiss to my cheek.

As always, Jayce has come bearing gifts. The same black bags from the text he sent me a few days ago now dangle from his fingertips.

"For me?" I quiz, an air of excitement coating my words.

Jayce is the one on my roster who I see the least, but he likes to spend the most. He works for an oil conglomerate that has him traveling all over the world, sometimes at a moment's notice. I never ask for a thing and that seems to make him want to spend even more on me.

I swear, *men and their logic.*

The last thing I'm gonna do is complain though.

My dad had to know what he was doing when he picked a name for me that literally has "princess" in its origins. He set me up to be spoiled from the start.

Did I mention that I don't like working? Money is just a tool I use to get what I want. And if it's somebody else's money, even better. As long as the soft lifestyle I crave is always available to me, I see no sense in changing anytime soon.

"Oman wasn't the same without you, Lulu," Jayce breathes against my ear before swiping his lips across my cheek in a chaste kiss.

I lean into the kiss and beam up at him as he transfers the bags to my hands.

Jayce smells so damn good. I try not to get lost in the scent as I eye him closely.

All six-foot-four inches of him. With his smoldering green eyes and lowcut Caesar, he looks as good as he smells. Even though he's overdressed, as always, in an immaculately tailored suit.

We are truly the living definition of "opposites attract." Jayce is a proud workaholic with too much money and not enough time on his hands. I'm convinced he'd marry his job if it was possible. Where I see leisure as a lifestyle, he *strongly* buys into hustle culture. Whatever makes him happy, I guess.

Our opposing outlooks on life is what drew him to me in the first place. We actually met at my winery, *Talulla Manor*. He was there on a group tour of the grounds with some of his colleagues and spotted me lounging by the on-site spa.

Thinking I was a guest of the bed and breakfast attached to the winery, he sat down beside me and started flirting with me. When I told him I owned the place, he hadn't been able to stop the fascination that was taking over his face.

"You'll come with me next time?" he questions, staring at me intently.

"We'll see," I answer. And it's the same reply he'll always get from me. He's never even set foot in my house and wants to know if I'll fly off to Western Asia with him. I like his optimism. But, no.

Trips imply a sleepover *and* seeing each other more than one day in a row.

I don't see myself breaking rules #2 and #4 for him in one fell swoop. No matter how *fine* he is.

7.
Talulla

"I'm happy your ass got stood up tonight!" my best friend Celeste all but shouts as we clink our shot glasses together.

I roll my eyes because I didn't *technically* get stood up. The date was already in session when things went left. A last-minute work emergency called Jayce away in the middle of dinner, so naturally I called CeCe to keep the party going.

Celeste and I met in high school and ever since then she's been down for our spontaneous antics—big or small.

CeCe met me at the bar across the street from the restaurant for a quick drink. That was nearly three hours ago. . .

"Ok, that's my last shot or I'm not gonna be able to walk tomorrow," I tell her. "I gotta tinkle then we need to call a car," I announce.

I tap the screen on my phone and see 01:33 staring back at me. The glare from the screen makes me squint.

Yea, I need to take my ass home. The bar is closing in half an hour anyway.

When I return to our little booth less than five minutes later, CeCe is smiling smugly at me.

"Our ride will be here in five," she chirps, her hand running over the tight turquoise curls atop her head.

Snickering, I ask her, "What? You called somebody that quick?"

I guess I'm not the only person ready to go home, I think to myself amused.

"Mhmm," is the only confirmation she gives me as she finishes the last of her mixed drink. "Let's go outside. Our driver will be here soon."

I don't miss the mischievous gleam in her eye, but my mind is on other things as she shoves my bag in my arms and steers us toward the door

"Wait, I have to close our tab!"

"Already taken care of."

"I'm gonna fight you, CeCe. I told you tonight was on me!" I wail as we walk outside, and the night air hits my face.

It's a welcome relief from the musty smokiness of the cramped bar.

"You'll get over it," my best friend shrugs dismissively, pulling her vape pen out of her back pocket.

"What color is the car you ordered for us and whose house is it taking us to?" I ask, curious about the details but not really caring. Wherever we end up is where I'm sleeping because I'm too tired to do otherwise.

CeCe gives me that smile again and I want to know what the fuck is up.

"White," she says around a cloud of blueberry scented smoke, only partially answering my question.

I get closer to her on the sidewalk, crowding her space.

"Your cryptic ass better be glad I'm too buzzed to ask any more questions. 'Cause you acting shifty and I don't like it." By now, my finger is wagging at her.

I sway on my feet a bit, completely ruining the moment.

Damn these heels straight to hell. This is why I live in sandals. *Flat* sandals.

CeCe giggles at my failed attempt at sternness then her face lights up, "Our ride is here!"

My back is facing the street, so I turn around and see a familiar pick-up truck pull to a stop at the curb.

"Since when does Pierre drive for CarPool?" I ask, referencing the one and only ride-sharing app that works in our neck of the woods.

I'm still frowning when he hops down from the driver's seat and rounds the front of the truck.

Butterflies dance in the pit of my stomach when he pulls both the front passenger and back doors open in one fluid motion. Always the gentleman, he waits for us to approach so he can help us climb into the monstrosity of a vehicle he owns.

"Let's go." CeCe grabs my wrist and tugs me toward the car.

"Why'd you call him?" I'm speaking through clenched teeth.

"He called while you were in the bathroom," she admits, wiggling her brows. "So naturally I answered and told him we needed a ride. Thank me later for making your booty-call easier."

I scoff at the air of confidence in her tone. CeCe swears up and down that any interaction we have is a prelude to something filthy.

I hadn't expected to see Pierre tonight. Especially not on the same night as my date with Jayce.

Admittedly, my first thought was to call Pierre when Jayce pulled the plug on our date, but I didn't want to use him as a stand-in.

I know for a fact he would have dropped whatever he was doing, but he's more than a backup plan so an impromptu girl's night it was...

We haven't seen each other since he dropped me off after the doctor's visit a few days ago.

Texts have been minimal, so I figured he was busy with work. I, personally, was keeping myself occupied with preparations for my demo lesson at the library.

I wasn't *actively* avoiding him. I guess it just worked out that way.

"Ladies," his deep baritone greets us. A smirk is on his lips as he watches me wobble a little in my heels.

"You good, princess?"

CeCe pretends to gag at the nickname, and I don't have the energy or coordination to elbow her in the ribs.

"Yup," I say cheerily and even *I* don't believe me. But it's not the alcohol causing this reaction. That's all him. His nearness has been having that effect on me lately. He helps CeCe into the cab of the truck first and then holds his hand out for me. I readily place my hand in his palm because there's no way I'm going to win against the footrail in these heels.

Electricity shocks me at the touch and I jump. I play it off by gripping his hand tighter.

The alcohol must be making me hallucinate. There's no way there were actual sparks. Right?

He sees me glance warily at the footrail.

"I got you," he whispers, and his voice is close to my ear. Close enough to make goosebumps erupt all over my very warm body.

Pierre basically has to pick me up and *place* me in the car. I'm not even mad. I relax against his soft leather seats and am looking through his center console for gum by the time he climbs into the driver's side.

I find the gum easily and pop some into my mouth. Maybe the act of chewing gum will distract me from all the other sensations assaulting my body.

"Want gum, CeCe?" I ask holding up the container.

"I like how you offering her my shit," Pierre grumbles, putting the truck in drive.

Ignoring the remark, I place a piece in CeCe's outstretched palm and turn back around to look out the front window.

Pierre tosses a water bottle in the backseat to CeCe and another one in my lap.

"Finish that before I drop your ass off," he orders.

CeCe snickers then mutters, "Yes, dad."

"Whose house are you taking us to?" I ask him. Since I never got a straight response from CeCe.

From my view beside him, I see Pierre's eyebrows dip in the center of his forehead but he doesn't look at me.

"I'm taking CeCe home first and then you."

"Oh," is all I manage to say.

CeCe smacks my shoulder from the backseat. "You could sound a little more excited. I know you wanted to see his grumpy ass. You talked about him all night," she reveals.

My jaw hangs open and Pierre finally looks over at me as we come to a stop at a red light.

"You were talkin' about me?"

"CeCe, count your days," I mumble, avoiding the urge to fidget when I feel Pierre's energy shift beside me.

It's so fucking weird. Some days I can neatly file him way into the best friend category and other days it's a hopeless cause. The lines blur and chaos of the sweetest kind usually ensues.

I ignore the self-satisfied smirk on Pierre's face as he makes a right turn onto one of the main roads.

The great thing about Belle View is that everything is only ten minutes away. Or maybe that's the bad thing about it. This town is small. Sometimes I think it's too small. It definitely explains why Pierre was able to get to the bar so fast.

Still, I stare out of the window mesmerized by the tree-lined streets as if I've never seen them before. I love my hometown and *most* of the memories I've made here.

In no time at all, we're pulling up in front of CeCe's townhome. I notice a light is on and a shadow moving behind the blinds.

I clear my throat obnoxiously.

Time for payback.

"Pierre, did CeCe tell you that she got back with Davina after you helped her pack up all that shit and move it?"

"You trollop!" CeCe kicks my seat from behind like a child and I can't help but laugh at her outburst.

Pierre turns to look at CeCe with his signature frown. "For real, Ce?"

I hear the back door of the truck swing open just as a figure appears on her front steps.

"Talulla, I'mma get your ass back," she threatens slamming the door and talking to me through my cracked window.

"What? I thought we were in a sharing mood tonight."

CeCe throws up her middle finger and walks toward her front door.

"Tell Davina we said heyyyy. Love you!" I shout out of the window.

8.
Pierre

"I'm hungry," Tally announces not even five seconds after I've pulled out of CeCe's development.

"The bar had food, why didn't you eat it?" I ask even though I already know the answer.

When Tally's drinking, there's only one food that she craves and not many bars specialize in grilled cheese sandwiches.

"Can we go to the diner?" she asks, eyeing me with big doe eyes. She knows exactly what she's doing.

It's two a.m. and the diner is conveniently open until four, making it the only place in Belle View for anyone to eat at this hour. Not to mention it's the only place aside from her own kitchen where she can get her grilled cheese made the way she likes it.

Wordlessly, I steer my truck in the direction of Gerrie's.

"If we go to the diner, I want something in return."

Her brow raises and a crooked smile pops up on her face.

I know her mind just traveled to the depths of the gutter and shake my head laughing.

"Get ya mind out of the damn gutter. I'm not trying to fuck for a grilled cheese, Tally." Besides, I wasn't trying to fuck her drunk anyway. I needed her sober or that shit wasn't happening.

She giggles in the passenger seat, her head falling back as she laughs. Finally, she calms down and looks over at me just as we pull into the diner's parking lot.

"I mean their grilled cheeses are *that* good. There's a lot I'm willing to do for them."

Despite the late hour, I notice that the place is packed. Peering over at Tally, I ask, "You want to get it to-go?"

Tally silently agrees with a nod, eyeing the crowd inside.

"So what do you want in return?" she asks once we're back in the comfort of my truck.

A Styrofoam container sits her lap and the only thing I got is resting in my cupholder.

"And why'd you order coffee? It's the middle of the night," she points out, frowning.

"Take a drive with me?"

With all the shit on my mind, it's probably how my night would have ended anyway. But now that I'm around her, I'm not really trying to say goodbye anytime soon.

Long drives have always helped ease my racing mind. And for some reason, I know having Tally in the passenger seat will only had to that effect.

"You're such a sucker for quality time, Pierre. I love it," she says wistfully, completely bypassing my question. A gentle smile is playing at her lips as she opens her container.

A goofy grin I can't hide erupts at her assessment. I'm reminded of the unsolicited lesson on love languages she gave me a few months ago. the details are grainy, but I vividly remember how *into it* she had been. And that shit was adorable.

"That's a yes?"

Tally slides me a glance, picking up her sandwich. "Only if I can control the music."

"Bet."

♥

Two hours later, Tally is beside me with her legs folded like a pretzel in front of her while she stares straight ahead. There's a slight break in the darkness that surrounds us as I steer us down a never-ending two-lane highway that connects Belle View to the surrounding cities in our county.

Aside from her playlist streaming through the speakers, we've been riding in companionable silence.

I know she's sobering up from her night out when she reaches for my forgotten coffee and helps herself to what's left.

"God, that's *awful*," she groans dramatically, before taking another sip of the black coffee. "How can you stand this every day? And don't give me that crap about it being an acquired taste."

"Then I ain't got shit to say since you know everything."

She snickers beside and falls silent for a minute. Out of nowhere, I hear her shift in her seat beside me before she asks me, "You ever think about leaving Belle View?"

"Where did that come from?" My hand tightens on the steering wheel while I wait for to follow it up with an explanation.

The odds of her asking me that today of all days has me on high alert. The interior of my truck is still dark enough to hide the involuntary frown on my face.

"Because I think about it all the time."

Her clarification somehow triggers both relief and more defensiveness than I want to admit. My frown deepens.

"Aside from college, I've never spent that much time away. I mean if we don't count the two years I lived with Lucas…but I drove home once a month so I didn't feel like I was ever really *away*."

I tamp down the irritation I feel at the mention of her bitch ass ex and ask what's really on my mind. "And now you want to change that?"

"Not really, but it doesn't mean I don't think about it. I always wondered why you stayed honestly. That's why I asked."

"I've never had a reason to leave." Well, up until today that statement was true.

"It was just a question," Tally fills in the silence, sensing the tension from my side of the car.

I don't know why I'm sure on edge, but damn it I am.

"I'm glad you never left. I like having you around. But I always wondered if you *wanted* to be somewhere else."

"I've never wanted to be anywhere you weren't, princess."

"Maybe you say that because you never met someone else, *somewhere else*."

That shit right there annoys the fuck out of me. Tally has this uncanny ability to completely bypass any confession of feelings or affection and turn it into something else.

I fucking love this woman and she's so set on erasing—or ignoring—any proof of that fact.

I cut my eyes at her, prepared to respond, but the look on Tally's face as she takes in the first glimpse of dawn stifles my response, melting my annoyance about being brushed off.

Horizontal bands of pink and orange fracture the sky closest to the ground, giving way to soft light.

A corn field is to our left while tobacco grows in the field on the other side of the highway.

A serene smile has inched across her lips as she leans forward, closer to the windshield, so that she can see the view on the other side of me better.

"Views like this kinda make staying worth it," she says with a hint of airiness. As I split my attention between her and the road, I can't help but silently agree.

♥

Around 6:15, I finally pull up in front of Tally's condo building and throw my truck in park.

She turns to me with a lazy smile that tugs at me and says, "Thank you for taking the scenic route."

Even though she managed to stay awake for the whole ride, I can tell sleep is only about a blink and a half away for her.

"Let's go inside," I say and only get half a nod in return before she's opening her door.

Inside her condo, I take the keys from her hand and place them on her entry table as she walks towards her bedroom.

Following close behind, I watch her drop onto the end of her bed. Her back hits the mattress as her feet dangle from the edge. I walk over to take off her shoes.

Listen, we've established that she's spoiled, but I never said I'm not *partially* to blame for that shit.

My hand brushes past her calf down to her ankle, and my dick instantly pushes against the confines of my boxers, the familiar softness of her skin triggering a reaction. But I smother the desire coursing through me as I start to unfasten the shoes.

Her eyes are falling closed by the time I look up at her again.

"Get up," I command, gently pulling her to the edge of the bed.

"I'm sleepy," she whines, scooting away.

"I know you are, but you got shit on your face so let's go wash it off."

"Pierre stop yanking on me before you dislocate something," she groans, rolling over face first into the pillow. Probably in an attempt to shun the bright overhead light I'd turned on.

With another firm tug, she's back at the end of the bed and scowling up at me.

"It's called makeup, Pierre. Not *shit*."

"Let's go," I command, pulling her by the wrist in the direction of the bathroom.

In the bathroom, I lean against the door as she begins to go through her routine.

"I got a question."

"What?" she asks, not opening her eyes as she continues to scrub her face damn near raw.

"What were you saying about me to CeCe all night?"

Her hand stills and she peeks at me in the mirror, blatant skepticism covering her features.

"Nothing good," she quips with a playful grin, clearly lying through her teeth.

"Yea, aight," I laugh.

Tally goes back to doing her thing and thoughts I don't want to entertain creep to the surface. I'm hit with the realization that nights like these won't exist if I'm gone. If I take my dad's offer and move away, the late-night drives will cease. I won't be the person picking her up from the bar when she's had too much to drink. And I won't be the person who gets to see like *this*. Fighting sleep, half-dressed and mumbling in the mirror.

I hate those thoughts and push them away. Far way. Because I don't want to lose this. Even when we're doing nothing it feels like everything. Because nothing is everything with her.

The peace I feel with her is unmatched and I don't know how the hell I'm going to replace that. I don't want to.

Greedily, I take a minute to stare at her face like I haven't studied it a million times before. Her heart-shaped face is smooth and doesn't give away that she's coasting towards thirty. No lines interrupt her soft skin. Her lips are full, two-toned, and pouty. Every feature on her face is perfectly crafted and I could probably write a poem about that shit at this point.

She is the perfect embodiment of everything I fucking love.

With hair I want to pull and lips I want to kiss every single second of every single day.

I could probably stand here and watch her for hours, but I move into action instead when she finally leans over the sink to splash water on her make-up free face.

Her eyes are glued to me as I grab her toothbrush and tube of toothpaste. I smear it on top of the brush and watch her out the corner of my eyes. The way she's looking at me has my dick hard. But I'm going to ignore it.

"Here," I say extending the toothbrush in her direction.

A soft expression passes over her face, but she remains wordless as she accepts it from me and begins brushing her teeth.

I wonder what that look was about as I walk into her bedroom to grab the satin bonnet she keeps on her bed post.

On my way back to the bathroom, my eyes catch sight of three matte black shopping bags. Bags from a luxury store that Tally would never shop at on her own. Bags from a store she *would* gladly accept gifts from though.

My fist tightens around the bonnet in my hand, the soft material crumpling in my hand. I feel my jaw clench. I don't know how long I stand there staring at them. Could be seconds, could be minutes. But I shake it off just as quickly.

Just another reminder, I think.

I know what it is and what it ain't when it comes to Tally. She's always been upfront about that.

That doesn't make the shit any easier to digest though.

"Here," I say when I make it back to the bathroom and see that she's finished brushing her teeth. The word comes out harsher than I intend, and I swallow the frustration jamming my throat to regain my composure.

If Tally notices, she doesn't say anything. Instead, she pulls on the bonnet and sends me a smile through the mirror. My face is too tense to return the gesture.

"Why are you so good at taking care of me, Pierre Bear?" she asks, turning around to wrap her arms around my torso.

And just like that, her touch and that stupid nickname eases the rigid tension in every part of my body. This woman is going to be the death of me. It can't be healthy to swing from these extreme emotions this quickly.

"I'm good when I know that you're good," I tell her honestly. It's just as much for her as it is for me.

She's still staring at me with an unreadable expression on her face.

"Why you looking at me like that?"

"You look good that's why," she volleys right back.

My mood lightens even more and I hear myself laugh.

"You flirting with me, Talulla?"

"Maybe," she says, shrugging and hugging me tighter.

"Ready for bed?" I ask, peering down at her. My lips brush her forehead, and she nods as I continue to shower kisses around the rest of her face.

I just don't kiss her lips. We're weird like that. We slut each other out on a regular basis, but unless sex is involved, we *never* kiss. Not because I don't want to. It's just another complicated aspect of her rules, so I respect it.

She's climbing into bed when I try my luck again, "What were you and CeCe saying about me tonight?"

Her smirk is immediate. She sinks back against her throne of pillows and regards me with a curious expression.

"Why do you wanna know so bad?"

I push a mirthless laugh past my lips at her avoidance.

Because I love you and I want to know if you feel anything close to that for me before I pack my shit and move away, I want to blurt out.

But I don't.

"You're so good, Pierre. So so good," she whispers with a faint smile.

Hearing that almost makes up for the fact that she's still dodging my question.

She's already falling asleep before I can form my next sentence.

Walking out of her bedroom, I hit the light switch and utter, "Good night, princess."

Back in my truck, I sit there and contemplate for what feels like hours.

If I move who's going to make sure she's straight on nights like this?

If I move how long will it take her to replace me?

The rational part of my brain knows that Talulla is attached to me. Hell, maybe she even loves me. In her *own* way. How deep that love goes, I don't know.

And it's that very uncertainty that's got my head fucked up.

9.

Talulla

He's watching me.

I can feel the heat of his eyes burning into me, even though he hasn't approached me. Yet.

When I agreed to accompany Jayce to the mayor's mansion for a benefit, it slipped my mind that Pierre was most definitely on the guest list.

Of course, he's here. His family practically owns this town.

He loves to downplay his status by saying he's "just a landscaper" but his family's bloodline runs deep in Belle View.

His father, Pierre Sr., opened Lancaster Landscaping Designs in the nineties. Since then, the company Pierre now co-owns with his siblings has held a monopoly on our beloved hometown and wins every major city contract there is.

Then, his father's big brother, Louis, owns Lancaster Logistics, a freight company that started as a modest trucking business in the early 2000s, but seems to grow larger by the second.

And last, but not least, his aunt Priscille—God rest her soul—founded Lancaster Interior Architecture and Design, a luxury home interior design studio now run by her two daughters.

Each business is housed in its own massive warehouse in the Lancaster Industrial Park. The same industrial park where my father now has headquarters for his construction company.

Anyway, the whole damn Lancaster family is black excellence personified.

And if I'm being honest, I'm a fan. But right now, I'm much more interested in the way Pierre's eyes are tracking my every move throughout the mansion. I'm even more impressed that I'm able to keep up a semblance of a conversation with Jayce while this is all taking place.

Jayce places his hand at the small of my back and pulls me closer to introduce me to yet another business acquaintance and I nestle into his side, thoughts of a brooding Pierre still at the forefront of my mind.

What's up with me running into him on more than one of my dates in the past month?

Up until recently, I'd done a damn good job at keeping him far away from my suitors. Not only because of his possessiveness but because of his annoying penchant for telling me that all of my dates were subpar.

Speaking of subpar, the glass of white wine in my hand has me wishing I'd stuck to water.

By the time I excuse myself to the ladies' room, my cheeks are sore from the polite smile I've had painted onto my face all evening.

I drop my unfinished glass of wine on a passing waiter's tray and relax my face as I walk down the portrait-lined corridor towards the bathroom.

I don't even need to use the facilities, but I'm desperate for a minute alone. A minute where I'm not performing as the perfect arm candy to a man I barely see once a month, if that.

Exhaling, I pull a tube of lip gloss out of my bag and observe myself in the ornate, gold rimmed mirror.

The bodice of the dress I'm wearing is shimmering in the dim light of the small bathroom, but I still smile at the pretty navy-blue material.

I smooth my hands over the fabric, loving the way it hugs my curves and one side opens to a slit, exposing my right leg to the mid-point of my thigh. It gives the illusion that my short legs are much longer than they are.

With my legs on display, I chose a pair of silver stilettos to accentuate the look. A pair of stilettos that are currently killing my feet. What I wouldn't give to be barefoot right now.

But *beauty is pain*. At least that what Pierre's mom, Gwendolyn, says. She's the one who helped me pick out everything. Of course, she was ignorant to the fact that her son would be gawking at me all night while another man paraded me around the mayor's mansion.

Pierre. I can still see the smug look in his eyes and the knowing smirk on his face as he lifted his glass of whisky at me from across the room before taking a sip. All night he'd been taunting me without getting too close and it was the cruelest form of foreplay I've ever had to endure.

Trying not to drool as I watch his thick fingers flex around his glass. Trying not to swoon when I catch sight of his perfect teeth every time he smiles at someone. Trying not to linger whenever I am in earshot and hear the smooth timbre of his deep voice.

It's all maddening, especially since he seems intent on letting me be. Something I would usually be grateful for but am now feeling an odd sense of loss over. The absence of our sometimes-chaotic encounters is making this night feel longer than it is.

Without warning, the door of the bathroom pushes open and Pierre stalks inside like he belongs here.

Speak of the devil.

His presence surrounds me instantly, wrapping around my senses and making my knees quiver. The pulse at the base of my throat skyrockets, but I maintain a cool appearance. Like it doesn't bother me to have him crowding me in such a tight space.

I keep applying my lip gloss like everything is normal. It's not the first time we've found ourselves in the same bathroom. We've been friends for almost twenty years and honestly, weirder things have happened.

Meeting his eyes in the mirror, the mix of annoyance and hunger in his glare makes me nearly drop the tube of gloss.

I brace my hands against the sink just in time, steadying myself when all I want to do is crumble at his feet.

He looks so fucking good, too.

Dressed in black from head to toe, the only exception is his signature chain resting at the base of his thick neck. Visible veins make his throat look a little too tempting and kicks the throbbing of my own pulse into overdrive.

He inches closer to me, until his front is pressed firmly to my back.

"Why didn't you lock the door?" Pierre's voice is heavy and rough with an emotion I can't name but can definitely feel.

"I just came here to get away from the crowd," I confess. "And to freshen up." I wave the lip gloss in the air as proof.

"You wanted me to follow you, didn't you?" he jeers, his lips grazing my ear and eliciting an involuntarily gasp from me.

Quickly, I pull myself together. Well, I try to at least.

"From the way you keep popping up on my dates, I'm starting to think you're stalking me."

His eyes flicker at the absurdity of my statement, seemingly not at all amused by my attempt at a joke. He invades my bubble more.

Dropping his head near mine, he breathes me in before branding my neck with a kiss.

"That's Jayce?" he asks, his hands running over the bodice of my dress and up towards my bra-less chest. His thick fingers brush against the thin material of the dress and he lets out a guttural sound when he feels my nipples straining against it.

I'm an idiot for not wearing pasties.

Still thrown by the question, my head reclines against his chest, allowing him full access to my neck. I feel drunk after being in his presence for less than a minute. More stimulated in this short span of time than I have been by my actual date all evening.

My reaction to him is a clue that I clearly need serious help, but I don't want it right now.

Right now, I just want to keep feeling what he's doing to me.

Well, my body wants that. My brain knows I need to put an end to this before Jayce realizes I've been gone for too long. Or before someone starts pounding on this door.

"Pierre, we can't do this here."

"What exactly are we doing, princess?" His teeth graze my neck and I lose it, squirming against him as my body fights a losing battle with my head. One prioritizing pleasure while the other is preoccupied with decency.

Inhaling sharply, I turn around and fall right into his trap. Instantly, his hands replace mine at the edge of the sink, caging me in.

Damn it.

My chest is heaving from the heavy breaths I'm taking and it's all I can do to meet his eyes.

His expressive orbs burn into mine, a wicked mix of adoration and entitlement lingering in the depths. I know right then that all hope is lost.

How am I supposed to deny him anything when he looks at me like the sun rises and sets just for me?

"You want to go back to him?"

Hell no! I yell inwardly, but my lips say otherwise. "Yes."

Pierre gives me an indolent smirk as soon as the lie touches the air. He looks so irritatingly cocky. So self-assured when I can barely remember what day it is right now.

"Pierre, I have to go." But I don't want to go anywhere. He knows that just as well as I do.

So, when he licks his lips and speaks again, I shouldn't be surprised.

"I love that dress, princess." I would take his compliment at face value, but his words are tinged with desire, a ravishing glint entering his unwavering gaze.

I suck in another sharp breath. "Pierre, I have to g-"

"You taste as good as you look?"

My mouth snaps shut at his question, loss for words as he pushes his hips into me.

"Let me make you come." He leans in to press a whisper of a kiss against my lips. The joining of our mouths is over way too soon. And then he's watching me again. "You come for me and then I'll let you go back to your little date."

Oh. My. Fucking. God.

It's a deal straight from the devil if I've ever heard one.

Pierre nips at my bottom lip with his teeth, not so patiently awaiting a response that's suspended in my throat.

"Can you do that for me, princess?"

10.

PIERRE

My words shock the hell out of her because she immediately turns around and faces the mirror again. She stares at my reflection through the glass and shakes her head slightly.

"Why you turn your back on me?" I ask with a teasing smirk. I know exactly why.

"Because you've lost your mind. I'm on a *date*, Pierre."

"Fuck that gotta do with me?"

Tally's eyes tell on her, darkening to a deep espresso shade as she tucks a tube of something into her purse.

"You're impossible."

"That's fine, I can eat it from the back," I murmur, my hands anchored at her hips as she sucks in a sharp breath.

"Pierre."

"That's what you want?" I graze my teeth against her neck and smile when she trembles. "Talk to me, princess."

"I shouldn't but I do," she whimpers. That's all I needed to hear.

On their own, my hands start traveling over her hips and further down. The high split exposing her right thigh makes it easy for me to slip my hand up her dress and discover the lace thong she chose for the evening.

"Pierre, I--"

She doesn't get to finish those words as my fingers cup her sex, absorbing the heat there. Feeling my effect on her strokes my ego and makes the front of my pants even tighter.

I've been hard as a fucking rock since the moment I watched her walk in.

But my dick can wait. The satisfaction I get from making her come will be worth it.

With that thought in mind, my fingers graze the material of her underwear again before fully pushing them aside.

My eyes are locked on hers in the mirror as my hand comes in contact with her bare pussy, the evidence of her arousal leaking onto my fingers.

"Tally, you're wet as fuck."

All I get in return is a low whine and her clamping her eyes shut.

"Fuck, baby. It wasn't my plan to fuck you in this bathroom but you're making it hard," I confess, my words wrapped in a double entendre.

"Pierre," she hisses out as my middle finger begins to massage her clit. The tight ball of nerves is slick as I spread the juices from her slit around it.

Her eyes are still closed so I graze my teeth against her bare shoulder and tell her, "Open your eyes, princess."

"I can't," she whines.

"Why not?"

"Because if I look at you, I'm going to come."

Her voice is strained as I continue to rain kisses across her shoulder and up her neck.

Gripping the edge of the sink, she looks blissed the fuck out. Even with her eyes closed. Pride bubbles up in my chest.

It's all the ammunition I need to abandon the teasing strokes and slip two fingers inside of her.

The familiar warmth of her pussy has me fucking rigid and straining even more against the zipper of my tailored pants.

As my fingers start to work in and out of her, the sound of her labored breathing joins the soundtrack of her wetness announcing her arousal and coating my fingers with every movement.

I swear, every time I retreat and push back inside, she's wetter than the second before.

Tally throws her hips back and moans my name again and I know she's getting lost in the assault of sensations I'm hitting her with. My teeth at her earlobe, my hand digging into her waist, the fingers of my other hand buried deep inside of her.

Wanting to add to the sensory overload, I make sure to pull my fingers completely out of her every few strokes and massage her swollen clit with the wetness drenching my fingers. Each and every stroke designed to bring her closer to orgasm.

"Pierre." By now, she's panting, her eyes finding mine in the mirror as she continues to wind her hips back into my groin creating more friction as she chases her first release.

"What, princess?"

"Why are you doing this to me?" she groans out, her eyes falling shut again as I feel her tightening around my fingers before a series of contractions take over her body.

I relish her release like it's my own and give her neck an open-mouthed kissed before answering her question.

"Because I can," I tell her, plain and simple. And it's the fucking truth.

I know the effect we have on each other, and I don't mind exploiting that shit every now and then. Even in the bathroom at the mayor's mansion.

Before she can come down completely, I drop to my knees behind her and gather the material of her dress in one hand. Holding it against her hip, I kiss the perfect round globe of her cheeks before I use my free hand to push her legs apart.

"Bend over," I order, my voice deeper than I recognize. Thick with lust and another emotion I won't name right now.

"Pierre, please, I need a minute," she mewls, trying to catch her breath.

My hand lands against the ass I just kissed, and a loud smack rings out in the small space as my palm makes contact with the soft skin.

"Bend. Over."

This time, she follows my command. Her ass is angled up just slightly, exposing her slit from behind and clearly marking the target for my greedy tongue.

Leaning forward, I inhale her scent greedily before my tongue darts out and finally gets a taste of what I've wanted all night.

I devour her, my tongue ravenous as I bring her to another orgasm. I lick up the evidence of her nut as she continues to whimper above me.

My face is buried deep in her cheeks, and I'm tempted to start eating her ass when a loud ass knock interrupts us, making Tally jerk forward.

Unfazed by the interruption, I drag my lips over her asshole and press a kiss there.

I'm all set on my next mission when another knock is followed by a deep voice.

"Lulu, are you in there?"

Gasping, Tally reaches back to push my head away from her.

I move my head back, but I don't stand up. So when she turns to reprimand me, my face gets up close and personal with her pretty pussy. I lick my lips as if I wasn't just feasting on her less than a minute ago.

"Lulu." That damn voice breaks the spell though and I stand to my feet, dropping the material of her dress as I do so.

"Who the fuck is Lulu?" I growl and I know there's a matching scowl on my face.

She puts her index finger up to her lips in an attempt to quiet my voice.

"Shh," she says before turning her head towards the door.

"Jayce, I'll be right out. Give me a second."

"Are you alright?" he asks.

Fuck this nigga.

Tally rolls her eyes. Whether the gesture is towards me or his question, I'm not sure. Either way, the action makes me grin deviously.

"I'm fine. Can you go get me another drink? I'll be right out."

Her voice is high-pitched and if she'd used it on me, I would have known right away *exactly* what she was up to before speaking.

Jayce must be a little thick in the head because all he does is agree and finally stop knocking.

Tally sighs in relief. That doesn't stop her from cutting me a look to convey her annoyance though.

"Pierre. I swear to god, one of these days…"

I know she wants to get on me about almost blowing her spot. But I have more important shit on my mind besides her warning.

"Nah, why you let him call you that shit?"

The fuck is a "Lulu?"

Tally purses her lips and reaches over to grab tissue from the roll of toilet paper near the wall.

Taking it from her, I easily move the dress aside and shove her legs open just enough to clean up the mess there. I pull her thong back in place, unable to resist the urge to run my hands over her lips through the material. She shivers, pulling a smirk out of me as I smooth the material of her dress over her hips once more.

I can still feel her juices coating my beard but I'm not in a rush to clean her off of me.

When I look up again, her gaze has softened as she looks up at me.

There's something in her eyes that I can't pinpoint in the moment.

"What?" I ask, tossing the tissue in the trash can.

She's trying her damnedest to mask her reaction, but I catch her flushed skin and blown pupils while she looks at me trying to fix me with a reprimanding scowl.

Cute.

Tally breaks eye contact and shakes her head. "Nothing. I have to go."

11.
Talulla

"Lulu, are you okay?" Jayce is right at my side before I can make it to the end of the hall.

He extends another glass of that awful white wine in my direction. But this time I don't think twice before gulping it down in a single swig.

"Yea, of course," I answer, pushing the glass back in his direction. And to my own ears, my voice is a dead giveaway.

Jayce looks far from convinced as his green eyes rove over my face, searching for clues. He takes my now empty glass and pulls me into his side with his hand strategically placed at the small of my back.

I shiver at the contact as vivid images of what I'd just been doing flash in my mind's eye.

Taking a deep breath, I try to erase the memory of Pierre staring through my soul, his beard glistening in my juices as I brushed past him and stumbled toward the door.

Guilt pierces my bubble of composure and leaves me feeling deflated as I allow Jayce to lead me back to the main room of the event. But he pauses before we enter.

"Do you want to call it a night? I can take you home," Jayce offers still trying to read the expression on my face.

Instantly, I shake my head. "No, let's stay."

Honestly, I've never wanted to do anything less. But the only thing I can think of that would be worse than staying is going home to deal with the guilt ripping my insides to shreds.

♥

"Wait, wait, wait," my cousin Davina says above me as she works on retwisting my locs. "So you're still doing this weird dance with Pierre?"

After giving her a very tame summary of what happened last night, I can imagine her mouth is agape. But I can't see it because she's hovering over the back of my head working away.

"Weird dance is one way to describe it, I guess," I huff, folding my arms across my chest.

Our "weird dance" has been leaving me flustered lately. No, flustered isn't even the word. Last night had torn me apart.

Once I finally got home, I'd raced to the shower and scrubbed every trace of Pierre from my body. Well, I tried to. It didn't work. And it also didn't help that he was blowing up my phone the entire time.

I can't believe I let him do that to me in the bathroom while my date was on the other side of the door looking for me. And the worst part is, I had enjoyed it! At least in the moment.

Why am I suddenly feeling guilty every time Pierre and I have a "moment?"

It wasn't even that I'd let him devour me while I was on a date with another man—a discussion for another day—it was the fact that when I looked in Pierre's eyes after, I saw every feeling he had confessed for me. And then some.

That look terrifies me. But it makes what I have to do a little easier. There is no orgasm worth hurting my best friend more than I already have.

Right?

Right.

"Why you sitting there looking like your puppy just ran away?" CeCe asks, seeming to materialize out of thin air.

The last time I checked, she was on the balcony putting together a hammock. Now, she's standing directly in front of me.

"Davi twisting your hair too tight?" she pries, eyebrows dipping as her hands fist at her waist.

CeCe absolutely *hates* being left out of the loop and is about to barrage me with more questions until Davina answers for me, bringing CeCe up to speed as she continues to work on my hair. I tune them out as my mind continues to do cartwheels.

"So, what's the problem?" CeCe asks abruptly.

"The problem is that I'm starting to feel guilty," I confess pathetically. Thankfully, I'm not looking for sympathy because CeCe just rolls her eyes.

"Guilty why? I thought this is what you wanted."

"I wanted sex," I remind her. "*Not* this guilt every time Pierre tells me he's in love."

She thinks about that for a minute and shrugs. "So, what are you going to do?"

"If I knew that, I wouldn't be distraught enough to ask for advice while Davina is clearly trying to twist my thoughts," I groan.

CeCe chuckles and looks up at her girlfriend. "Babe, I told you that you were twisting too tight."

Davi huffs above me. "Tender-headed and tender-hearted," she snickers before going back to work. "Anyway, there's nothing wrong with having options."

"Exactly and if sex is all you have to offer then I see no problem with that," CeCe chimes in.

"Sex isn't all I *have* to offer. It's all I *want* to offer." I don't mean to sound defensive, but I hear it all over my tone. I sigh and try again. "I was cool with the attention, but I don't like the thought of someone getting hurt because of me."

"How do you know someone has to get hurt?"

"Right," CeCe co-signs. "Pierre is a grown ass man. If he continues to show up for the shenanigans, then everything must be fine."

She makes it seem so easy. And maybe if it wasn't Pierre, it would be that simple.

But every time I look into his eyes lately, I feel like we've passed the point of no return and that scares more than anything has scared me in a while.

12.

PIERRE

The next time I see Talulla, it's two days later and she's limping through my parent's front door with my brother, Marcus, at her side.

I would be alarmed at the sight if it wasn't so fucking common.

Two summers ago, Marcus and Talulla had the bright idea to start an adult flag football team and play for it.

Every week one of them comes back in this house with a battle wound because they refuse to accept that they aren't as young as they used to be. I can almost bet money that today is no different.

Still, my innate protective instincts for Tally kick in. And before I know it, my legs are carrying me away from my post on the couch and towards the two of them.

"What happened?" I ask, my eyes running over her frame. She's wearing the team's t-shirt and a pair of grass-stained gym shorts. The belt containing one flag is still resting lopsidedly at her waist. Shaking my head, my eyes fall lower until I see the purplish bruise on her swollen right ankle.

Instant anger replaces my usual calm.

"What the fuck, Marc? What'd y'all do to her?"

Clearly put off by my harsh tone, Marcus scoffs at me.

"Man, you know Tally don't listen for shit. Parts of the field were being redone and we were told to avoid that area. But she wanted to run down on the other team at practice. And tripped and fell in a hole in the middle of the damn field. Ain't nobody touch her."

Relief rushes over me just as quickly as amusement. I can't help my smirk when I look Tally up and down a second time.

Her lips are pressed together as she rolls her pretty amber eyes at my brother.

"Please stop talking about me like I'm a five-year-old. I'm right here! How was I supposed to know that patch of grass had a false bottom?!"

Annoyed with the both of us, she throws her hand up and starts limping away when my mother appears.

"I wanna know who the hell is doing all this damn cussing in my house."

"Sorry ma," Marcus and I apologize in unison, neither one of us brave enough to call out the pot calling the kettle black. Gwendolyn Lancaster doesn't play that shit.

Not expecting to see Tally, her voice and gaze soften immediately after we speak.

"Hey, honey!" My mother takes in Tally's disheveled appearance and swollen right ankle. "What them people do to you this week?"

Tally starts a play by play of what happened as they disappear down the hall towards the dining room.

I lock eyes with my brother and notice how run down that nigga looks. "Wore your ass today huh?"

"Man," he smacks his teeth with a shake of his head. "I plead the fifth."

He backs toward the staircase and turns away to climb up to his old room, no doubt to shower.

I go in search of Tally and find her talking with my parents in the dining room.

"So you're saying you wouldn't have carried me off the field?!" Tally's voice is an octave higher as she finishes the question on a laugh.

She's sitting in one chair while her right leg is elevated on the one adjacent to her.

"Girl, I ain't throwing my back out fooling with you. I would have called you an ambulance though," my dad tosses back at her, handing her an icepack.

The way she loves my parents and the way they love her back will never get old. She's got them wrapped around her finger, too. They dote on her like their lives depend on it.

Suddenly aware of my presence, Tally grins up at me from her chair. "Your dad says he's making his famous ribs for me."

"I already planned to make these ribs, little girl. What I *said* is that you can have some if you're still here when they're done in a few hours," he clarifies, leaving the room to get to work in the kitchen.

Tally waves a hand at him, her smile working its way around my heart like a vice grip.

"Semantics," she mumbles under her breath, drawing a chuckle from me and my mom.

♥

An hour later, I'm kneeling in front of a freshly showered Tally as she sits at the foot of the bed in my old bedroom.

"I'm starting to think you enjoy making me serve your ass," I grumble, wrapping her ankle in Ace bandage. She's dressed in one of my old t-shirts and a pair of sweats.

"Don't act like you don't love it," she deadpans. "I don't *make* you do anything."

She ain't fucking lying.

In the last two weeks alone, I had undressed her and put her to bed, ate her out at a charity event and now this.

That stunt at the mayor's mansion had even shocked me, but something came over me that night.

I'd fought the urge to approach her all night and had almost won. Until…

Talulla looked edible in that dress and tasting her before sending her back to a man I knew would never have the privilege did something to me.

"What are you thinking about?" she asks, her hand at my shoulder as I finish securing the bandage around her ankle.

"Making you come while you were on a date the other night," I reply bluntly.

I stand to my feet, forcing her to look up at me.

Her breath hitches and the sick delight I get at rattling her is all too familiar.

"Pierre," her voice is sharp, and my name sounds like a warning.

"What?"

"Ay," Josh interrupts, appearing at the door. "Ma is sending me to the store for relish, y'all need anything?"

I watch as Tally's snaps her mouth shut, swallowing whatever she was about to say. Her eyes travel over to my brother who's watching us with a confused look on his face.

"I'll go with you," Tally blurts out, jumping to her feet.

Injured ankle forgotten, she almost falls backwards as soon as she puts weight on it. My arms catch her easily, pulling her against my front as she steadies herself by grabbing my arms.

"Careful." I wonder if she can feel how much my heartbeat accelerated when she crashed into me.

"Uh, you coming or not?" Josh asks from the doorway. His confusion is at an all-time high now as his eyes bounce between the both of us.

"Yup, I'm coming." Tally's voice is squeaky as she untangles herself from my hold and walks out of the door without a look back.

"The fuck was that about?" Josh asks me pointedly, watching Tally disappear down the hall from the corner of his eye.

I know he has questions. Hell, I do too. Too many damn questions and not enough answers.

All I can say when I make eye contact with him is, "It's complicated."

13.

TALULLA

This time when I walk out of the children's library, I don't falter when I reach the lobby. I don't panic at the sight of dutiful moms or joyful kids.

The news I just received has me floating in the clouds.

I got the guest storyteller gig and they want me to start next week. Every Tuesday and Thursday for one hour, to be exact.

I'm scared shitless but excited at the same time.

They said I blew them away with my demo by incorporating music time into the act.

Celeste and I had stayed up way too late making those paper towel and bean maracas, but it had been worth it.

I breeze through the sliding doors and speed walk over to my car. After I drop down in the front seat, I pull my phone from my purse. The first person who comes to mind is Pierre.

But I stop myself because what if I speak too soon? What if I suck at this and he wants to know how it's going later? What will I tell him then?

He doesn't even know I went after this opportunity because I swore CeCe to secrecy, and she actually kept her mouth shut for once.

I still can't figure out why his opinion means so much to me, but it does. I want him to take me as seriously as I take him.

I strum my fingers against the steering wheel as I watch people trickle in and out of the library.

We don't have to talk about this but I still want to see him. I pick up my phone again and mutter under my breath, "Fuck it."

♥

"Pierre," I whimper as the man beneath me avoids my grasp once again.

I'm straddling his lap, my knees digging into the softness of the mattress as I over his swollen erection. I'd chosen this position to be kind to my injured ankle but the sensations rippling through me from this friction are enough for me to never want to look back.

"Tell me what I wanna hear and I'm all yours, princess," he says calmly, like we aren't millimeters apart. On the verge of becoming one, but not quite close enough.

Huffing, I grind my wetness against him and watch torture play over his fine fucking features.

Good, I'm not the only who's going to suffer.

"Say it," he grinds out, looking up at me with a warning in his eyes. "Say it's mine and nobody else is touching you."

"You already know that," I whisper as my hips start moving on their own accord. Even though he isn't inside of me, rubbing up against him is building tension to a dangerous point inside of me.

The possessive fire in his eyes turns me on even more. As much as I fight his possessiveness, it's actually my favorite aphrodisiac. Especially when he knows damn well I'll never let a soul get as close to me as he does.

Desire crawls down my spine and twists a fiery ball in the pit of my belly, moving lower until the throbbing between my thighs is unbearable.

I want him inside of me. I *need* him inside of me.

"Fuck," Pierre grits out, his eyes darkening to a shade I've never seen before.

My hands rove up and over his muscular pecs. I inch them up to his toned shoulders before settling loosely around his neck.

His eyes flash dangerously at the position of my hands. I know he's tortured right now. And I love knowing that I'm the cause of it. Because I feel the same way.

I know he can feel me leaking onto his thighs, wetting his dick with my slippery arousal even though he's not inside of me yet. That's how much I want him.

His hands find my hips and his fingers dig into me without remorse. I gasp at the startling sensation of his grip on me. Until he drags me forward on his dick, teasing me while I'm actively teasing him.

"This what you want, princess?" he asks, his voice rough with desire.

"God yes," I cry out, not caring that he has reduced me to whining.

His hands still around my hips and this time he moves his hips, creating friction from below. Friction that makes me tighten my grasp around his neck.

Smirking up at me, he looks triumphant despite the position we're in.

He reaches between us and positions his hardness against the soft wetness of my opening.

"Tell. Me. It's. Mine."

Each word is annunciated coarsely, dripping with authority as he uses one hand to stop my moving hips and the other to hold himself rigid against me.

I can't take this shit anymore.

I'm going to come from anticipation alone if this goes on too much longer.

Finally, I open my mouth and say what he wants to hear. What he already knows but wants a verbal reminder of.

"It's yours, Pierre. Only yours." My words die out as he pulls me down onto him in one breath-stealing motion.

He's filling me, stretching me, controlling me from underneath as my hips begin to undulate against him, desperate to create even more contact.

"Ah, fuck," he moans and it's music to my ears. "Say it again."

His skin is hot beneath my touch as my hands fall away from his neck and find his chest again. I rock my body back and forth, slowly adjusting to the sudden fullness inside of me. My pussy welcomes him in, pulsing around his deliciously veined length as he thrusts in and out of me.

I will never get used to how good he feels inside of me. No matter how much time passes or how often we do this, it will never not feel like ecstasy. Heaven on earth. Pure bliss. Fucking nirvana.

Bouncing up and down on his dick is one of my favorite hobbies. The sound of my ass hitting his thighs every time I land will never get old.

"You feel so good, Pierre."

I rise and fall against him rhythmically, my hips swiveling and creating even more fire between us. Prickly pleasure overrides my system, making me forget everything except the feel of him inside of me, simultaneously making me stretch and contract.

My voice is hoarse when I utter how good he feels again.

"I know baby, I know."

The tightness swelling in my middle grows more intense as I continue to rock against him in pursuit of my first orgasm.

When Pierre notices the change in my breathing and feels my legs begin to tremble, he looks up at me with satisfaction shining in his light brown eyes.

"That's right, princess. You gonna come on this dick?" he asks, already knowing the answer.

I nod jerkily, my arms falling behind me to grip his thighs as I continue riding him frantically, chasing the nut that I know is going to shatter me in half.

"I love coming on your dick, Pierre."

He smacks his hand against my ass, the sting of pain competing with the mounting pleasure I'm feeling in other places.

Seconds later, my body locks as I come undone, my body reaching climax and tensing as I ride out the waves. Pinpricks of pleasure surge through me at lightning speed, momentarily robbing me of the ability to think about anything other than how damn good this feels.

"Shit," we both cry out in unison, as my pussy milks his dick for the orgasm he owes me.

Panting, I try to recover from the pleasure but don't have time to catch my breath before I feel him swell inside of me. He erupts with a grunt, spilling his seed inside of me. He pulls me down by my waist, pinning me against him so that I feel every spasm of his completion and every drop of his come filling me to the point of overflow.

The intense shudders and the stickiness between us only acts to drive me over the edge again. Without warning, I come again, my pussy convulsing and pulling the last of his orgasm from him.

"Got damn it, Pierre!" my words are laced with both accusation and praise. My lower body bucks against him, my knees digging further into the mattress on either side of him.

I can't catch my breath long enough before another flood of pleasure assaults me.

He hasn't even done anything extravagant. Just the fullness of him inside of me coupled with his unwavering stare has me in shambles. This man is going to be my end.

Minutes later, we're still tangled up in each other, my thighs burning from the workout and sweat slicking both of our bodies.

I pull my head away from his shoulder and stare down at him. The expression waiting for me takes my breath away.

From the earnest intensity in his gaze, I should know to expect his next words to be just as earth shattering.

"I love you so much, Talulla."

Stunned silence engulfs the space between us as I immediately avert my eyes. He reaches up and his forefinger turns my chin back in his direction.

"I know that's not what you want to hear right now, but I can't fucking help it."

He's right. It's not what I want to hear, because it derails my common sense every time. I don't get how three simple words can be so heartbreaking and soul-mending at the same time.

My nose tingles and while the sensation is expected, it's still unwelcome. I bite my lip as tears threaten to fill my eyes.

"Pierre." I shut my eyes at the sound of my voice cracking in half. The two syllables of his name sound strained and foreign.

I knew I shouldn't have sought him out. Nothing has felt right between us since the mayor's mansion fiasco. I should have known scratching my itch one last time would end in chaos and here I am, bearing witness to just that.

Opening my eyes again, I find Pierre staring up at me.

His eyes bore into mine, for once not providing their usual reprieve. Resolve darkens his normally kind gaze and I want to cower. His voice is as firm as his grip on my hips when he speaks again.

"I'm not going to stop until you love me, too," he vows.

14.
Talulla

"What do you mean you're avoiding him?" CeCe asks as we step onto the front deck of my father's house for Sunday brunch.

We stop at the bottom two steps, not yet ready to go inside due to the nature of our conversation.

"Exactly what I said. I'm not going to hang out with him for a while until I figure this out."

"Last I checked, "hanging out" wasn't the problem. It's the hunching part."

My nerves are still rattled after seeing Pierre last night. CeCe is *not* helping. Which is honestly on brand for her.

CeCe clucks her tongue at my prolonged silence, folding her arms across her chest. "This is insanity. He loves you, Tally! What's the big deal? Clear your roster and let him love you."

I don't point out that she's singing a completely different tune to what she said a few nights ago. With her wishy-washy ass.

"What are you so afraid of?"

Everything, I wail internally.

"It's complicated," I say instead.

Not to mention how on edge I feel because Pierre's house is right around the corner from my dad's.

CeCe grunts, rolling her hazel eyes at me.

I chew on my bottom lip, all too aware of her watchful gaze.

"What does he have to do? Prove it to you?"

That question makes my skin crawl.

"No, no one should ever have to *prove* their love. It's either there or it's not. This isn't about him proving anything, this is about me."

Me and my crippling inability to receive love.

CeCe nods in agreement but still sports a confused frown.

"So what the hell do you want, Tally?"

That's a loaded question. What *do* I want?

Finally, I start my response, "I want—"

Just then the front door flies open and my dad is standing there with a huge smile on his face as he looks down at us through the screen door.

"Girls! You made it! Come on in."

♥

I accept the mimosa from my dad with a grin and send CeCe a look across the table as she accepts hers.

She's batting her lashes at him like a fucking menace.

She always tries to flirt with my dad. Granted, he's a very handsome man. And not yet fifty since my parents had me so young.

But still!

It's unnerving sometimes. Not to mention, I'd already let her infiltrate my family when she started dating Davi. She needs to leave my dad out of this.

A mess.

"Stop batting your lashes at my dad," I say through clenched teeth once my dad has returned to the kitchen.

"Or what?" she asks boldly, taking a sip of her lychee mimosa.

"I'll snatch them off," I threaten, finally raising my glass to drink.

CeCe looks scandalized by my threat and bursts into laughter seconds later.

Before she can form a witty retort, my dad reappears with three very different plates of food.

"Brunch is served, ladies."

My mouth waters at the sight of the French toast and scrambled eggs overflowing on the plate that I know is mine.

CeCe's plate has waffles, while my dad's has toast.

He places the plates down in front of us and I start dancing in my seat.

"The day you stop dancing at meal time is the day I'll know something is wrong," my dad jokes at the familiar sight.

My love life may be in shambles but one thing I love unabashedly is food. Especially good, home-cooked food. My father's cooking is what I was raised on, but that's not the only reason I love it. Some people's parents can't cook to save their life, but mine is a damn good chef.

"No wonder you won't settle down with just *any* man. Look at how your dad still spoils you," CeCe mutters, craftily filling her mouth with food right after she says it.

At the mention of my dating life, my dad's ears perk up like a golden retriever hearing their human toss their favorite ball.

"Are you dating anyone worthy of your heart yet, cupcake?" he asks, smearing blueberry preserves over his toast.

Narrowing my eyes at CeCe, my annoyance deepens when I see the pleased grin on her face.

Meeting my father's keen gaze across the table, I shrug off his question.

"You'll be the first to know as soon as I am," I answer.

He gives a noncommittal "Mhmm" and keeps his incisive amber eyes on me.

My dad knows bits and pieces about my adventures in dating. Bare bones, skeletal knowledge, if you will.

He's aware that I prance around town going on dates from time to time. That information would be pretty hard to hide in a town the size of Belle View anyway.

But he doesn't know the details. And he definitely doesn't know anything about mine and Pierre's complicated *non-relationship*.

Not because I think he'd be disappointed. Quite the contrary.

From the time we moved in across from the Lancasters almost twenty years ago, he's loved Pierre and his brothers like his own sons. But especially Pierre.

I can't explain their draw to each other, but it makes sense. Kinda.

Come to think of it, they're a lot alike.

Both mild-mannered, hardworking, protective, and doting.

Yikes. The thought that I'm sleeping with a man who closely mirrors my dad's personality seriously makes me want to gag.

So, I shift the conversation to the work I've been doing at the library. I tell him all about the story times I've completed and how I plan to incorporate other elements like music into my future sessions.

The way my dad's eyes light up with pride makes my heart sing.

His smile is earnest when he reaches across the table to grab hold of my hand. "That's great. I know how much you loved that library as a child."

He stops as a somber look enters his eyes. I know exactly where his mind went.

Playing it off quickly, he squeezes my hand and states, "Those kids are lucky to have you, cupcake."

Hearing my childhood nickname only adds to the warmth I'm feeling. I'd had a serious obsession with sweets, especially carrot cake cupcakes, growing up. How my father had been able to keep me away from overindulging to the point of illness is still lost on me.

A fond smile lights my face as CeCe and my dad start talking about the latest happenings at her crochet clothing shop. She's talking animatedly about some of her new summer and fall designs when I zone out, caught up in memories of how we got here.

This was the house my father moved us to for a new start after my mother disappeared. Being in our old home had been too much for him. So, we ended up here in this split-level colonial. Right across the street from the Lancasters and their three sons.

Pierre's parents had moved to a different subdivision a few years back, but my father stayed put.

The construction company he started when I was in high school had really taken off while I was in college, giving him the financial freedom to do whatever he wants and go damn near anywhere.

He claims he never left because it was just him and there was no need for him to get a house with more space just because he finally had the means. So, he'd just renovated this place bit by bit until it was the most valuable property on the block.

Call me sentimental, but I'm happy he kept it. This place is home to a lot of good memories. Memories not marred by what happened in our other house.

And the greenhouse he built for me is still standing in the backyard. I'd probably throw a fit if he decided to move and had to leave it behind. I think he knows that too.

Cutting into my French toast, I smile tenderly at him as he patiently listens to CeCe explain something he will never understand about her crocheting technique. But that's Kendrick Evans. The most patient man I know.

I can't help but wonder why he's never tried to date since…everything. The judge had given him a default judgment in the divorce when my mom never showed up for the court appearance. No surprise there.

But he never speaks about love. I don't know if he does that for my benefit or his. I've always hoped he'd end up with someone who deserved him. He seemed more interested in other things.

To keep himself busy and to watch his money grow, he sowed his new wealth into multiple side ventures—one of which was the winery he gifted me on my twenty-fifth birthday. He told me he wanted me to have something in my name. I didn't understand it at the time, but now that I have the freedom to do whatever I want while the winery quietly finances my lifestyle every month, I get it.

"Everything alright, cupcake?"

I hear my dad's voice and my eyes dart across the table in his direction.

Realizing I'd zoned out entirely, I snap out of it and smile brightly.

"Everything is great, daddy."

A fond smile lights my face as CeCe and my dad start talking about the latest happenings at her crochet clothing shop. She's talking animatedly about some of her new summer and fall designs when I zone out, caught up in memories of how we got here.

This was the house my father moved us to for a new start after my mother disappeared. Being in our old home had been too much for him. So, we ended up here in this split-level colonial. Right across the street from the Lancasters and their three sons.

Pierre's parents had moved to a different subdivision a few years back, but my father stayed put.

The construction company he started when I was in high school had really taken off while I was in college, giving him the financial freedom to do whatever he wants and go damn near anywhere.

He claims he never left because it was just him and there was no need for him to get a house with more space just because he finally had the means. So, he'd just renovated this place bit by bit until it was the most valuable property on the block.

Call me sentimental, but I'm happy he kept it. This place is home to a lot of good memories. Memories not marred by what happened in our other house.

And the greenhouse he built for me is still standing in the backyard. I'd probably throw a fit if he decided to move and had to leave it behind. I think he knows that too.

Cutting into my French toast, I smile tenderly at him as he patiently listens to CeCe explain something he will never understand about her crocheting technique. But that's Kendrick Evans. The most patient man I know.

I can't help but wonder why he's never tried to date since…everything. The judge had given him a default judgment in the divorce when my mom never showed up for the court appearance. No surprise there.

But he never speaks about love. I don't know if he does that for my benefit or his. I've always hoped he'd end up with someone who deserved him. He seemed more interested in other things.

To keep himself busy and to watch his money grow, he sowed his new wealth into multiple side ventures—one of which was the winery he gifted me on my twenty-fifth birthday. He told me he wanted me to have something in my name. I didn't understand it at the time, but now that I have the freedom to do whatever I want while the winery quietly finances my lifestyle every month, I get it.

"Everything alright, cupcake?"

I hear my dad's voice and my eyes dart across the table in his direction.

Realizing I'd zoned out entirely, I snap out of it and smile brightly.

"Everything is great, daddy."

15.
Talulla

Closing the storybook on my lap, I look out at the children gathered around me.

Their smiling faces are full of wonder and amazement, feeding my ego just a bit. I know I just crushed that story-time though and their expressions are all the confirmation I need.

It's officially the end of my second week as a guest storyteller and I'm having the time of my life.

I'm still not exactly sure why I felt called to pursue this at this point in my life, but here I am. It probably doesn't help that Pierre is always telling me he thinks I'd work well with kids.

Something I had brushed off for years. Look at me now.

The kids here are some of the smartest I've ever met, and they make our designated half hour together fly by. I read to two groups every time I'm here for a total of one hour. It's the easiest, most fulfilling thing I've ever done.

One of my favorites, Leoni, beams up at me as the other kids scatter about the library with their parents preparing to leave.

"Ms. Lulu, that's my favorite book!" she exclaims practically falling forward into my lap.

I'd chosen to go by the nickname, Lulu, because it was short and much easier for most of the kids to say.

Grinning at her enthusiasm, I pick up the book and stare at the cover feigning amazement.

"Really?" I gasp. "I had no idea!"

In reality, I know she loves this damn caterpillar book and had decided to end our session today with it because of that fact.

Her reaction alone is all the reward I need.

"Yea!" she says, her blue eyes lighting up with glee. "My mommy and daddy read it to me every night!"

The look of pure satisfaction on her face fills my heart with joy.

Leoni starts telling me all about caterpillars and their life cycle until her dad shows up to collect her.

I watch their exchange. How she launches herself at him with open arms, confident in the fact that he's going to catch her and my heart soars at the picture they paint.

Being around kids multiple times a week has really gotten me pondering on the possibility of kids in my future. My *distant* future, but still…

It's an idea I toss around from time to time, but because of my stance against marriage, I always brush it off, telling myself that a kid deserves a *loving* two-parent situation. It's the least I could give my offspring after how things turned out for me.

Truthfully, I can only see myself having and raising a kid with one person. The one person I happen to be avoiding right now. We can barely get through a conversation without me running for cover, yet here I am thinking about kids…with *him.*

Lord help me.

Not ready to go down that rabbit hole, I shove the thoughts away and start cleaning up the reading area.

After a quick chat with Birdie about next week's game plan, I journey through the library and outside to find my current distraction's car parked at the curb.

Isaac's been asking me out more lately and I think I'm finally warming up to him.

The conversation is great, especially when he wants to discuss work and I know he'll always take me somewhere interesting and fun. We're never chained to a dinner table staring at each other bored.

When it's all said and done, I get to walk away from tonight with a nice meal and a few hours spent walking around at a classic car show.

I pull open the passenger door to his sports car and get inside.

Turning in the passenger seat, I take in his light wash jeans, his hoodie, charming eyes and ready smile. He's like a stock image representation of the word handsome.

"Isaac, honey. You're a sight for sore eyes."

His smile is slow and reveals the cutest dimple in his right cheek.

"I'm always happy to see you Tally," he returns, grabbing my hand and brushing a kiss against the top of it.

Delighted to have a distraction from my raging thoughts of Pierre, I pull on my seatbelt and look out of the windshield as people pass by.

"Ready when you are."

16.

PIERRE

～✕～

The Rink is smoky and dimly lit as usual. But being here brings up memories from some dormant place that make me seek out the reason I'm here in the first place.

I watch as she rounds the rink on her custom skates, a peaceful smile on her face. Oblivious to my watchful gaze, she grabs CeCe's hand and lifts their joined fingers in the air between them.

It's only then that I can confirm she's wearing shorts. A 2PAC t-shirt three sizes too big is swallowing her frame and hiding the hem of the shorts in question.

The tattoos covering her entire left thigh are on full display as she continues to weave through the sea of bodies on the skate floor.

She looks so damn good. Almost good enough to make me forget the reason I'm here.

It's been a week and a half since I've seen Tally one on one. She's playing the avoidance game and I'm losing my shit.

I knew I'd be met with some resistance after what I said, but a week and a half? She's trying to kill me. And that shit is lowkey working.

It's the very reason I'd hunted her ass down and I'm not leaving until we have words with each other.

Stepping up to the waist high wall separating the carpeted area from the skating surface, my eyes zero in on her again, unwavering until she feels my gaze on her.

I witness the exact moment she realizes that I'm here.

The smile slips from her face and she looks at CeCe with accusation written all over it instead.

I want to laugh but hold my pensive expression until she starts skating toward me. My heart starts racing, in direct contrast to the stoic expression on my face.

Tally comes to a dramatic stop in front of me, spinning 360-degrees before her hands brace against the wall between us. She leans forward, trying to catch her breath.

"Pierre, what are you doing here?" Her words are breathy, a fine sheen of sweat coating her forehead as her amber eyes take me in.

She's out here having the time of her life while she ignores my calls. Wild shit.

My orbs clash with her defiant brown ones, and I'm annoyed that she holds this much power over me. Yet, at the same time I'm secretly loving it. It makes no sense. If anyone had told me my kryptonite would end up being this five-foot-four spitfire with too much sunshine in her smile, I probably would have laughed in their face.

But here I am.

Addicted and losing my shit because I haven't touched her or heard her voice in ten days.

Fucking insanity.

I move closer to her, the scent of the oil she uses on her locs permeating the air between us and invading my nostrils.

She smells like home.

My hands join hers on top of the wall between us, my palms covering hers easily.

"Tired of running from me yet?"

Her lashes flirt with her cheeks and she tries to look innocent.

"I don't know what you're talking about, Pierre."

"Yea, aight," I say, inching even closer until I'm crowding her space. Even with the short wall between us, I can feel heat radiating off of her.

"You missed me?"

Tally's eyes are coy seconds before a challenge enters her stare. "Hmm, maybe."

My reaction is so immediate I don't even have time to think about it. I reach up and cup her chin before my hand slides down and covers her beautiful neck. My fingers missed being there. I flex them one by one around the column of her throat.

"Don't test me, princess," I warn her.

A devious smile is my only reward. She even reaches up and covers my hand with her own. But she doesn't pull it away. If anything, she increases the pressure.

God damn.

Her head tilts back even more. Like a silent invitation begging me to keep doing what I'm doing. "Oh look," she says quietly, teasingly. "My favorite necklace."

Did she really just say that?

My dick rises to attention, confirming what my ears heard.

"For fuck's sake, we're in public." I don't know if I say that for her sake or mine.

She flashes me another triumphant smile crushing any illusion of resolve I thought I had.

God, I love this woman. With everything in me.

"You're the one with your hand around my neck," she shoots back, a devilish twinkle in her eye.

Her tongue darts out to wet her bottom lip and I watch it all like a depraved fool.

"Looks like you're the one who missed me," she taunts as my hand finally falls away from her neck.

Eyes that had been watching us closely suddenly fall away. I just wanted to see her. It wasn't supposed to turn into us being a source of entertainment for everybody else.

For the first time since she skated over to me, I seek out the person who helped me time my arrival just right.

CeCe is sitting on one of those ugly ass carpeted benches on the other side of the rink, staring at us. Her glare holds something akin to annoyance and disbelief.

From her posture and gaze, I know I'm going to hear all about my piss poor execution later.

"How're things going with Kayla?" Tally asks out of the blue.

My eyes narrow at her. A stubborn look greets me in return.

"Don't do that."

"Do what?"

"Try to create distance between us. I haven't seen that woman since the night we ran into you at the museum."

Tally looks contemplative at my words.

"Hmm, that's too bad. She seemed perfect for you."

Is this what she's been doing while she avoids me? Creating bullshit excuses for us to not be in close proximity because she's scared of the truth in my words?

"Why are you dodging me, princess?"

She won't meet my eyes, letting me know I'm right. She comes up with an excuse anyway.

"I've been busy."

"With *who*?"

Tally looks amused and shakes her head.

"You mean with *what*. My life is more than men, you know."

For whatever reason, I'm soothed by her cryptic answer. It's a little comforting to my ego to know there hasn't been some wannabe replacement swooping in trying to steal any more of her attention.

But why is she being so damn secretive?

"What's going on with you, Tally?"

She looks at me and I can see her debating on whether to tell me the truth or not.

Instead of giving a straight answer, Tally resorts to what she does best: distracting me.

"Come skate with me," she invites, her hips already swaying as she artfully disentangles herself from my hold.

I watch her skate off and wonder if I won that exchange or not.

Probably not if I have to think about it.

♥

"Lord, it's hard being the only one in this friend group with a lick of sense," CeCe groans as we slide into a booth at Gerrie's Diner half an hour later. Treating her to dinner was the consolation prize she'd requested for getting Tally and I in the same room. However briefly that may have been. Talulla disappeared shortly after our run-in, saying she needed to go to her dad's house for something.

"I got sense," I bite back, grabbing the menu to hide my smile. CeCe's irritation was always funny as hell and fake as fuck. She couldn't be mad at anybody to save her life. She just likes to talk shit.

"Lies you tell," she mutters under her breath. "I stuck my neck out for you and then you show up on some caveman shit! Now Tally's mad at me and we were supposed to go to the Manor tomorrow for a spa weekend. If she cancels, I'm gonna be on your ass."

She's pointing an impossibly long nail at me. I always wonder how she manages to crochet with those claws...

But them taking a trip to the bed and breakfast Talulla owns catches me off guard. Talulla Manor has been hers for the last four and a half years but she's hardly there.

I start to wonder if she'd planned the trip to get further away from me or if it's just a coincidence that she's going. I catch myself in that thought and shake my head.

Everything doesn't revolve around you, asshole.

Feeling on edge at the thought, I flex my fingers but then I instantly remember them being wrapped around Tally's neck and I'm right back at ground zero.

I decide to use my dinner companion to my advantage, since the meet-up we orchestrated went sideways.

"Celeste, be real with me."

CeCe narrows her eyes at the sound of her full name and looks around the diner as if to see if anyone heard me.

"Why you calling out my government name like that? You don't know who's in here!" she hisses from across the table.

Jesus Christ.

Why did I pick two of the most dramatic women I know as best friends? And why the hell did I fuck around and fall in love with one of them?

Her antics make me roll my eyes before I try again. "Anyway, keep it real with me."

"What?" she looks agitated by the question, much more interested in checking the menu she's seen a hundred times before.

"Do you think this thing with me and Tally can work out?" Regardless of what she says, I already know I'm not giving up, but maybe it's my tactics I need to change.

Something in my voice must have caught her attention because she drops the menu and starts tapping her nails against the top of the table while fixing me with those intense hazel eyes.

"Of course," she shrugs. "I personally think she's crazy about you whether she admits it or not."

A smile tugs at the corners of my lips. *Crazy about me, huh?*

"But you know like I do, that Tally has plenty reason to be resistant. She's been burned. Once by her mom and then again by Lucas. She doesn't want to get hurt again and I honestly get that. It's the reason she got all those damn rules. And you know how she feels about those rules."

Deep in thought, I lean back and regard her with half a frown on my face.

"To be honest, I'm starting to get tired of her damn rules," I speak truthfully.

CeCe snickers but looks sympathetic, "Yea, well good luck."

17.
Pierre

"Hey, ma."

I bend down to kiss the shortest member of the Lancaster family. My brothers and I have towered over since we were in middle school.

"Hey, Peanut." Her smile takes over her face when she greets me.

I grin, hearing my nickname and enter the house fully, heading straight for the kitchen where I hear the most commotion. The aroma coming from there is another factor pulling me in that direction.

My dad and Josh are standing around the center island with beer bottles in hand.

"What's up, y'all?" I greet even though I saw them both less than an hour ago at work.

The three of us fall into a conversation about an upcoming fishing trip until my mother enters the kitchen, joining us to check on the roast she's making in the oven.

With that done, she slides off her oven mitt and fixes me with a frown.

"Where's Talulla been hiding herself these days?"

"I don't know, ma," I mumble and cut my eyes at my dad who makes a dramatic show of kissing his teeth.

Here we go.

Either my mother doesn't realize my father's theatrics or she's too focused to comment.

"I haven't seen her in a while." Her frown deepens.

Both of my parents adore Tally. But they have two very different understandings of our relationship.

In my mom's eyes, Tally is still the sweet little girl from across the street. She loves her like the daughter she always wanted and never had—because after popping out three boys back-to-back, she'd thrown in the towel. So, Tally's entrance into our lives had been a point of solace for her. Most days I love their bond.

What I *don't* love is the look she's giving me right now. Like she's blaming me for Tally's absence without fully knowing what's going on.

I slide my father a glance and his lips are pursed like he's got a secret. I snicker.

The whole thing is comical in my eyes.

"What did you do?" my mother asks, fisting her hands at her thick waist.

"Dang ma, how you know I did something?"

Her eyebrow raises but her lips stay zipped. Somehow, her message is still loud and clear.

"We're in a tiff right now," I finally admit.

Her response is almost immediate. "What's that got to do with me?"

Josh and my dad both laugh, and I cut my eyes at them. Ain't shit funny.

My mother is folding her arms across her chest when I look back at her.

"She can't come say hi just because y'all got beef?" It's her turn to suck her teeth. "Tell her I want to see her narrow behind. And sooner rather than later."

"Yes ma'am." I just concede, knowing there's no point in arguing with her.

"I'd tell her myself, but you know I don't know how to work those damn phones," she huffs leaving the kitchen, probably to continue watching Family Feud until dinner is ready.

Left alone with my brother and father, I hold up my hand before they can utter a word.

"I don't want to hear it."

Josh takes the warning in stride, lifting his hands in surrender before taking another swig of his beer.

My father, on the other hand, clearly wants smoke.

"You know, PJ. Whenever you—"

"What's happening, y'all?!" Marcus calls from the hallway, interrupting my father's unsolicited advice.

I've never been happier to hear my loudmouth brother than in that moment.

With my youngest brother stealing the show, I slip out of the kitchen and toward the living room to chill with my mom. One of the many perks of her being in the dark about Tally and I is that she never pries. And I can use that right now.

♥

"How's shit going with you and Tally?"

After dinner, I ended up alone with Marcus because Ma gave us both dishes duty. How Josh and my father escaped this is beyond me.

I close the dishwasher and glance over at Marcus who's standing at the sink cleaning the larger pots and pans.

For some reason, I've always been more open to discussing deeper shit with him than anyone else in my immediate family. Even with him being younger than me, the nigga can be surprisingly wise.

"Same as the last time we talked."

"Still no communication?" He sends me a curious look as he rinses out the pan in his hand.

"Nah, we saw each other and talked." Vivid images of the skating rink play in my mind.

"Damn, and nothing changed?" he sounds doubtful. For good reason.

This is probably the longest Tally and I have gone without talking since we've known each other. She's scared and I get that, but it's starting to look bad. I don't know why I was so damn confident about being able to work against her fear in the past.

I'm starting to believe that I'm batting out of my league here. The confidence I felt talking to CeCe just a day ago is a thing of the past. The more I think about it, the more doubt I have.

I tell Marcus about my failed attempt at a confrontation to fill him in and competing sympathy and amusement shines in his eyes.

"Ah, I see."

"See what?"

"You ever notice that you have issues with control?"

Frowning, I lean against the island and stare him down. "Elaborate."

My youngest brother shrugs and turns off the faucet, turning to face me.

"It's just something I've noticed. I don't know if it's because you're a middle child trying to prove yourself or if it's because you're just wired that way, but you seek control in a lot of situations. You always find a way to have the upper hand. And people usually yield to you."

I ignore his dig about being a power-hungry middle child. I care more about the other shit he said.

Again, I invite him to elaborate.

"Anyway, Tally is not one of those people. She doesn't yield to you, and I think that's the biggest problem you're having with this. Instead of finding a middle ground or going over to her side, you want what y'all have to look a certain way and it's fucking with you big time that it doesn't."

I turn that thought over in my head a few times.

Fuck. Why did he have to make so much sense?

"Listen," he says when I don't respond verbally. "You've always known what it was with Tally right?"

"Yea."

"You knew about her rules. You knew that she wasn't looking for a conventional relationship, right?"

Where the hell is he going with this?

"Yea," I say anyway.

"You knew all this and still chose to get involved. I get that you love her, but you know just like all of us that Tally loves her freedom. She always has."

It's irritating how right he is.

"She is who she's always been. That's probably why you fell in love with her."

Right again.

"So you have a few choices when it comes to moving forward."

"Which are?"

Marcus shrugs again. "Letting go."

My brows bunch up in the center of my forehead, and he starts talking to cover his tracks.

"Not in the way you're thinking. I don't mean let go of her entirely. Although, I guess that's always an option."

He chuckles at the scowl on my face. I'm glad one of us can laugh about it.

"But what I really mean is releasing the expectations. Letting go of your desire to get her to come around to your way of thinking. Letting go of your need to win her over and have her confessing the feelings you already have. Maybe *you* having those feelings is enough. Shit, maybe there's nothing else you need to be doing right now besides letting her process that and *come to you*. Let her seek you out when she's ready and go from there. Release control and just be open to what could happen."

"And let her choose some other nigga?"

That sounds like a strong *hell no*.

"Do you really want to end up with someone who doesn't choose you?"

Shit. When he put it like that...

"You don't have to take my word for it though. Just know that this isn't something for you to "fix." I know you get high off the feeling but it's aight to chill sometimes. You're not wrong for loving her, bruh. But you do have to take responsibility for the way you act on it. In this case, the way you *act out*. When you stop forcing shit, sometimes better stuff can happen."

Hell, maybe he's right. But my mind still can't come to terms with the idea of letting Tally go. Not after everything. My brain won't wrap around the idea that maybe we aren't even going to end up together.

"I mean, another option is actually doing something about it." Marcus shrugs. "And don't think I'm trying to contradict everything else I just said. By now she knows you love her. But what do you want her to do with that information? Beyond saying she loves you back," he adds just as I'm about to answer.

I pause to think. Really think.

"If she confessed her love for you right now, what would be the next step? Are you telling her that because you want her to stop seeing other niggas? Do you want to date her exclusively? You trying to make her your girl? Your wife? What's the actual outcome you're looking for aside from that lovey dovey shit?"

He gave me something to think about. What *is* the next step?

I clap Marcus on his back and head over to the fridge for another round of beers. "Why the hell are you working at a landscaping company? Sounds like you need to take your ass back to school and become a therapist."

Laughter meets my words. But I'm dead serious.

"I'm curious though," he says after I hand him a beer.

"What's up?"

"If you're planning to move, why does any of this matter anyway?"

"That's actually what I wanted to talk to you about."

18.
TALULLA

A couple's massage with Celeste will always the answer to almost all of life's problems.

After arriving at the manor, our overnight bags were taken from us, and we were escorted directly to the boutique spa on the grounds.

It felt good being here. Although I rarely made the trip, I always felt at home when I showed up.

And I *always* showed up with Celeste. She's my rider and I know she enjoys the spa perks as much as I do.

Outfitted in plush robes embroidered with the winery's logo, we're both sitting on the end of our massage tables feeling drowsy after the ninety-minute session.

We're also both sipping a glass of white wine. Definitely not helping the drowsiness, but anything goes this weekend.

"Girl, I feel like jelly after that massage. I didn't know I was that damn tense," CeCe muses.

I drain the rest of my wine glass and finally hop off the table.

"Come on, let's go get ready for dinner. Anthony says they are going to prepare all the new additions to the menu."

Before arriving, I set up a dinner date for us on the balcony of the executive suite where we are staying.

There is a communal dining room for all of the property's guests, but privacy is a necessity for the things I want to talk to CeCe about this weekend.

We exit the spa and step onto a cobblestone walkway leading to the courtyard. A group of tourists are huddled on the other side receiving a tour of the property, a typical sight for Fridays and Saturdays.

Talulla Manor is not only a bed and breakfast but a winery with a full in-house winemaking operation. Tours are offered every weekend to give guests an up-close view of the process. From our fermentation tanks to the aging facility and finally the bottling line. Guests get to see it all.

The only thing we don't do is grow our own grapes, but we do source them locally from nearby vineyards.

Each tour is capped off by a wine tasting in the courtyard and I can tell that's what's happening now.

CeCe and I scurry along the walkway without being seen and make it to our room to shower and get dressed for the evening.

I'm actually looking forward to this friend date more than usual. We haven't spent intentional time together in a long time. At least it feels like a long time.

Between her being busy with making stuff for her store and her relationship with Davina, CeCe's free time is hard to come by. Couple that with the fact that my life has been one long loop of me simultaneously avoiding and being consumed by Pierre lately. Yea, we're way overdue for a "spill" session.

An hour later, we are doing just that while we fangirl over the spread in front of us. The chef really outdid himself and I plan to tell him as much before we leave Sunday morning.

"Aight, let's cut to the chase," CeCe speaks, her eyes watching me over the rim of her glass. "How much longer do you plan to play this game of cat and mouse with Pierre?"

I'm in the middle of stabbing the leaves of my salad when my hand stills. I drop my fork and meet her eyes.

"I'm not *playing a game*," I wail at her. "I'm legitimately terrified, CeCe!"

"Okay, chill. Save the theatrics, I ain't him," CeCe grumbles.

I cut my eyes at her, and she gives me a teasing look of her own.

"CeCe," I whine. I don't have time for her to be taunting me. Things have been so…different with Pierre lately and I don't know what the hell to do about it.

"I know, I know," she says reaching across the table to grab my hand. "Shit has been intense lately, huh?"

"Just a little," I admit, squeezing her hand. I find comfort in the contact and keep her hand in mine. CeCe is the least affectionate person I know so I'm going to revel in this.

She huffs out a breath and drops her fork, too.

"Well, I don't see you maintaining this distance too much longer. Look at you, you're stressed the fuck out. What are you going to do?" she asks directly.

"I don't know," I answer truthfully. If I knew what to do this trip wouldn't be necessary.

"You know Pierre's stubborn ass is not going to give up," she warns, picking up her glass again. "Do you even want him to?"

Deep in thought, I look out over the grounds of the manor and sigh at the beauty of the landscape. I couldn't have picked a more peaceful backdrop for this chaotic conversation. The twinkling stars lend me solace as I turn over the options in my head.

I definitely have to do something about Pierre. There's no way around that. Our friends-with-benefits situation is officially a dead zone. And I'm beginning to regret having started it at all.

Not the Pierre part. I could never regret him. But we are speeding towards disaster if something doesn't change soon, and I'm stuck on what change that needs to be.

Pierre says he loves me. Is *in love* with me. And all I want is to believe him *and* believe that I'm worthy of that love. But I am nowhere near that mental milestone.

"He says he's in love with me," I say, fidgeting with the tablecloth. "I feel so bad, CeCe."

"Why?" I can hear the frown in her voice.

"I don't know what to do when someone says they love me. I don't know how to believe them," I clarify.

This time when I look up, I see understanding and sympathy in her eyes.

"Do you *want* to believe it?"

"Yea," I say without hesitation.

"You answered that pretty quickly for someone who usually runs from these situations."

I slide her a shy smile that makes her chuckle. "There's something about Pierre. His resolve is really convincing even if I can't see what he sees in me. I want to."

"Listen." Celeste squeezes my hand again. "Even if Pierre wasn't in the picture, I need you to understand that you are a bad ass bitch who deserves a bad ass love. I'm sorry the assholes in your past ruined that concept for you, but you still deserve it. From the right person. It's up to you to decide if Pierre is that right person. Because his sprung ass definitely thinks you're *his* right person."

Finishing the wine in my glass, I stare at her.

"I know you're scared, and you have reason to be. But nothing that happened in the past was your fault and nothing you could have done would have prevented it. That much I can give you. It *is* on you to heal from it so you can experience love the way it's supposed to be."

She pauses to wipe her mouth with the linen napkin. After a sip of wine, she continues.

"I'm all for boundaries but your rules are rigid, and I think you know it. No one has a chance in hell. I'm also not opposed to dating multiple people at a time, but you don't even like those motherfuckers. They're just distractions. So, the ball is in your court, girl. Figure out your shit so you can love somebody correctly."

Her words are a direct echo of what I've been thinking for months. I need to figure my shit out.

"You're right."

CeCe nods, content with my reply.

"You'll figure out something that works for you. The same way you did with this place," she says, looking around. "You knew you didn't want this much responsibility so you hired someone to handle it."

"Too bad I can't hire someone to deal with this."

"It's called therapy, bitch."

I laugh from deep in my belly.

"Seriously, have you thought about going back? I know you were going to deal with all the stuff with your mom but a lot has happened since then. Maybe going back could help you make sense of this thing with Pierre. He deserves some clarity too. Even if it's not what he wants to hear. This back-and-forth shit is getting old though. I know y'all are exhausted."

I *am* exhausted. Therapy would be more effective than all the avoiding I've been doing. Because even though I've been avoiding the problem, it hasn't gone anywhere. It's just gotten worse.

"Sometimes I wish you didn't make so much sense."

CeCe smirks at me. "I'll never get tired of hearing you admit that."

Shaking my head, I grab the bottle and refill both of our glasses.

"Enough about me. Tell me what's going on with you and my cousin. And please, spare me the explicit details."

CeCe rolls her eyes at me before she breaks into an update about her on-again, off-again boo, Davi. I'm listening but my brain is working overtime trying to come to terms with everything on my heart.

By the time I crawl into bed that night, I'm tipsy and tired. But I know exactly what I need to do when it comes to Pierre.

19.

Pierre

I pull into the familiar driveway and cut the engine. The radio keeps playing because I haven't opened my door and the weather report catches my attention.

A low-pressure system has been identified off the Gulf Coast and is currently being watched in case it forms into anything stronger and heads towards land.

Damn, hurricane season seems to creep up faster and faster every year around here. The price we pay for year-round sunshine is being smack dab in the middle of Hurricane Alley.

My next thought is Talulla. She hates storms of any kind. And I hope for her sake that shit doesn't make landfall. At least not near us.

I also selfishly pray it steers clear of our neck of the woods because of the extra need for labor it'll create at work.

Already aware that Mr. Evans isn't home, I bypass the front porch and walk around the side of the house towards the greenhouse he built himself for Talulla.

Her fascination with plants had started at a young age and he'd done everything he could to cultivate it. Most of her favorite plants—some of which she's had for years—are housed in the A-frame greenhouse on her father's property. Others have made the migration to her apartment, but a lot of them are still here.

I need to quickly check on the tomato vine her father asked me about and then I'm headed to my brother's house for a kickback, where they'll no doubt grill me about whether I've decided to move and—

Talulla.

As soon as I step into the small eight-by-ten-foot space, my eyes land on her.

Standing there barefoot, in a skirt that touches her ankles and a top that barely reaches her ribcage. Her entire midsection is bare, revealing those strings full of beads I love to tug on in different contexts. Her hair is wrapped up in her favorite old T-shirt, forming a pineapple at the top of her head. I only know that term because of years of having her and Celeste as my friends.

Her back is to me and a watering can is in her hand as she hums along to the music in her Air Pods.

This is the first time I've seen her since the skating rink. That was three days ago, and I know from the post CeCe made this morning that they got back last night.

Talulla doesn't have social media outside of her business page for the winery, so I had to piece together the crumbs I'd been given.

A small smile touches my lips as I continue to watch her water her plants and hum off-key. Wrapped up in her aura like I always am, I don't even notice when she turns around until it's too late.

If Tally is surprised to catch me gawking at her, she doesn't show it.

Instead, she sends me an easy smile and removes one of the Air Pods from her ears.

"Hey."

We speak at the same time, producing an even wider smile on her pretty face.

She's the first to speak again.

"I'm glad you're here. I wanted to see you."

Hearing those words shouldn't be as heart-stopping as it is, but my heart begs to differ.

Tally walks closer to me and peers up through her long lashes, reminding me of our height difference. I maintain my silence since she appears to be in the talking mood.

"I even went by your job looking for you earlier. But your dad said you'd taken the day off."

This is all news to me. I find it ironic that I'd spent the better part of two weeks trying to track her ass down and then the moment she came looking for me, I wasn't around.

Ain't that some shit?

"So, I ended up eating lunch with Marcus and Josh," she shares, igniting jealousy within me.

Because whenever Tally shows up at the office, she always comes bearing food. I'm irritated that I missed it.

Neither one of my brothers had even taken the time to send me a text gloating about it.

Assholes.

I'm still stuck on the fact that she went searching for me.

Clearing my throat, I stare at her standing in front of me and feel what I always feel when she's this close: love. Unadulterated. Sickening. Head over heels type shit.

I remember our last encounter and pull down on the bib of my hat. Just because I love her doesn't mean I have to act *barbaric*. CeCe's words, not mine.

Anyway, she has a good point. There are other ways to get what I want without acting like a caveman.

I need to be gentle yet persistent. Let her come to me in her own time.

CeCe's suggestion mixes with my brother's warning.

I can't believe I'm taking fucking dating advice from CeCe *and* my brother. I must be desperate.

I want to laugh off the thought but a knot forms in my throat.

I *am* desperate when it comes to Talulla.

Which is why I open my mouth to apologize. Except Tally starts speaking first.

"I wanted to find you and apologize. Face to face." She's still looking up at me. Eyes wide. Surprisingly she doesn't reach up to twist the locs near her ear.

Hmm. Interesting.

I'm so caught up on her body language that I almost miss the gravity of what she said.

"Why are you apologizing?"

"For avoiding you," she says simply. "I was wrong for that. If you had done it to me, I would have lost my mind. We usually talk every other day and then I just disappeared. I'm sorry."

Until now, I didn't realize I even needed to hear those words. But the apology definitely relieves some of the tension I've been carrying around the last couple of weeks.

"I get it," I say, accepting her apology in my own way. "And I'm sorry for the way I acted at the rink. I shouldn't have come at you like that."

There's a playful smile on her face as she shrugs. "Honestly, I didn't mind it."

Remembering the words we exchanged during that very brief encounter, I smirk. I guess it's not surprising to hear that she didn't mind the theatrics since she had definitely played into them on her end. She always loved being manhandled.

We stand there for another minute, staring at each other silently until a smirk tips up the corners of Tally's lips. She looks like she's holding in a laugh, and I want to know what's so funny.

"What?"

"I missed you," she says, finally giving in to the smile. It transforms her face and ignites something inside of me.

I missed that fucking smile.

Suddenly, my hands are itching to touch her.

It feels weird to have been in the same confined space with her this long and not put my hands on her.

I fix all that and reach up to cup her chin in my hand.

"I missed you too, princess."

"And you forgive me?"

Like that was a real question.

I couldn't think of many things she could do in this life that I *wouldn't* forgive.

She's waiting for my response, but her arms are already encircling my waist. It's like she was waiting for me to initiate physical contact before she made her move.

The thought makes me smile.

"Yea," I say, kissing her temple. "You're forgiven."

"Good, because I want to talk to you about something else."

Pulling away, I study her face and the worry marring her causes *me* to worry.

Dread enters my bloodstream and I'm almost afraid to ask my next question.

"What is it?"

20.
Talulla

"No?" I frown. "What do you mean no? It wasn't a yes or no question, Pierre."

In fact, what I'd just said wasn't a question at all. More like a definitive statement.

"That doesn't change my response." The words are spat out as a scowl claims his face. "No. *Hell no.*"

Confusion marches in and my frown is pure instinct. I look up to meet his gaze.

His previously gentle countenance has withered into a caustic glare. I feel like someone just punched me in the gut. Hard.

It hadn't been easy to conquer my nerves and tell him that we should stop sleeping together.

But as much as I hate confrontation, I knew it was a conversation that needed to be had. And I was fully prepared for *some* push back, but not the look of disgust and damn near loathing I see directed back at me.

"I didn't realize things would get this complicated when we crossed that line last summer."

I'd been in a serious *drought* when we fell into our arrangement a year ago. Not for lack of options but because my jaded heart hadn't let me find any man worthy of my body. Pierre was –and still is—the only man who didn't make me cringe at the thought of being touched *like that.*

Pierre laughs but there's no mirth in the sound that rumbles from his throat. "Me being in love with you is what you call *'complicated'*?" He uses air quotes to punctuate his words.

"Pierre." His name is more of a plea at this point. A plea he doesn't care about.

"You want to cop out and act like nothing ever happened," he surmises all too knowingly, nodding his head as if he had cracked the code.

I suck in another breath.

"How the hell am I supposed to go back to being just your friend when I've had you leaking on my tongue? Huh? When I've been inside of you *raw*? Friend?" he scoffs, shaking his head. "Fuck out of here, Talulla."

"Pierre, I never planned for it to go this far. You know I can't do attach--"

"Don't finish that sentence," he warns. "Don't open your mouth and recite one of your fucking rules at me like I don't know them all by heart. Like I didn't try to walk on eggshells to make sure we didn't cross the arbitrary line *you made up* because you're scared of love."

His words feel like a slap in the face, but it doesn't mean he's wrong. A tidal wave of guilt drowns my next words. Instead, I fold my arms across my chest and bite down on my bottom lip to hide the quiver there.

Our reconciliation from ten minutes ago seems like ancient history now.

I know he must feel blindsided but leading him on had never been on my agenda. How was I supposed to know he would profess his love for me and actually mean it? No one had ever meant it in the past.

Which is exactly why I didn't know what to do with the evidence of his love. Unlike the others, he wasn't just talking. The love is *right there* in his actions, in the way he looks at me, in the way he cares for me. It's all too foreign. Too much.

And I feel like shit because that kind of love deserves reciprocity. Something I don't feel like I'm capable of doing. It's not his fault. This is all on me.

Opening my mouth to apologize, I promptly close it again at a sudden loss for words. It's never been hard for me to talk to Pierre. He's practically an extension of me. A permanent fixture in my life that I flow with like water. But right now, words escape me. And I feel worse.

He doesn't deserve the hurt in his eyes.

"Pierre, I'm sorry for the way I approached this. Confrontation is not my st--"

"Just another thing you can't do, right?" His voice is cold, void of any other emotion except anger.

Again, I try to open my mouth, but no words fall out and I'm sure I look like a fool standing there with my mouth hanging open.

"This is why you were hiding for two weeks? So you could work up the courage to say this shit? I knew you were up to something lately; I just didn't know it was this." Anger is replaced with disgust as he sweeps his eyes over me in a cold manner.

He has never looked at me like this before. I didn't even know he *could* fix his features to form an expression of such utter contempt.

"Be real with me, are you ending it with me so you feel better about moving forward with one of them other niggas?" The ticking at the base of his jaw is a dead giveaway that he's strung pretty tight, ready to pop at any moment.

"What?" I feel desperate to explain, all the while knowing he won't believe a word I say. "I'm not *ending* anything Pierre. I just don't want to lose our friendship and I feel like I'm leading you on the more we keep doing this and that's not what I want."

His light eyes rake over me, cool in their assessment. "You know damn well our friendship ended the day you let me fuck you."

This is news to me. But maybe I *am* delusional. This whole time I'd maintained that we were still the best of friends. Who sometimes fuck each other's brains out.

I realize now just how fucked up that sounds.

Delusion. Yea. That has to be it.

"So what now, Talulla? You used me for sex until you felt good enough to move on to someone else?"

The accusation in his tone breaks me in half. There's no way he believes that.

"Pierre, I wasn't using you!"

Nothing close to belief passes over his face and I'm stuck grappling for words once again.

"You know what Tally? Go be with whoever you think deserves you. It clearly ain't me and I'm not going to force you to try and see it my way. I'm done with this shit."

Panic settles in my throat in the form of a knot at those words.

I'm done.

What does that even mean? He can't be done with me. Not completely. I won't believe it.

"So you're saying we can't be friends?" The thought alone is enough to shatter my heart. There's no way he actually means that. Twenty years of friendship is a lot to throw down the drain over this. Isn't it?

There's no way he's prepared to do that. But the look he gives me says otherwise.

Why isn't this going the way I imagined?

Pierre backs away from me, his head moving back and forth in what I have to believe is disbelief. "I'm saying we can't be anything."

21.

Pierre

Last Summer

Talulla hovers over me in a stance I'm becoming all too familiar with these days.

Arms folded under her chest, pushing her cleavage up and out, right at me.

Maybe that's not exactly what she intends but it's where my mind goes. It's where my mind always goes when I'm around her.

This fucking "crush" I'd developed senior year of high school never went away. Even when my brothers told me it would.

If anything, it got stronger the more time I spent with her. Which makes this whole arrangement that much harder.

Ever since I got out of wisdom tooth surgery three days ago, she's been at my house bossing me around with the aftercare notes the dentist gave her clutched firmly in her fist.

Any shred of annoyance I felt slipped away a long time ago. I'm getting too much of a kick out of her telling me what to do like she runs shit.

"Are you in pain?" she asks, frowning at me.

"No, Tally I'm fine."

"Do you want me to order you more mashed potatoes?"

If I eat another mashed potato, I'm gonna throw up. Real shit.

"No. Come sit down," I say pointing to the couch cushion beside me.

"Or maybe I can have a smoothie delivered. You haven't eaten much today and I--"

"Tally, please. I'm not hungry, and when I am I can get my own food."

Her lips turn downward in a dejected frown. I almost feel bad because I know she's just trying to help. But like I told her, I'm fine. The pain killers they gave me have me coasting right now.

Having her in my house nonstop for the past three days has been unexpected but mostly pleasant. I knew that she wanted to make sure I was good, but unaware of just what that meant to Tally.

Apparently, it meant surveillance. Around the clock.

I'd love to see her little ass running around here if I'd had major surgery. She'd probably be unrecognizable.

Relaxing onto the sofa beside me, Tally releases a deep breath and pretends to focus on the TV. But I know her mind is racing.

This is confirmed when she looks over at me, a glimmer of concern shining in her eyes.

"I just want you to be comfortable, Pierre."

"As long as you're beside me I'm comfortable, Tally. There's nothing else you need to do for me."

A skeptical look flashes in her eyes, but she eventually nods and turns back to the TV.

She has no idea how much time I spend fantasizing about a day where we're on the same page and my fantasy is realized. Unfortunately, I know that day will never come. Her aversion to serious dating has been solidified since finding out her bitch-ass ex got married to someone ex while they were dating.

That was four years ago. And here we are.

"Fine for now, but I'm still going to make you something to eat before I leave tonight."

Lost in my thoughts about her being open to dating me, I almost miss what she just said.

"Leave?"

She's been sleeping here in the guestroom the last three nights and the thought of that ending sends anxiety racing through my blood.

I've gotten used to her being here and I don't want it to end. Even though I know that it means more to me than it'll ever mean to her.

Tally meets my eyes and looks surprised at whatever expression meets her. I school my features into what I hope is a neutral look and try asking again.

"You're leaving?" I question, dreading the answer.

"I'm sure you're tired of me by now," she says, winking. "Three days is way longer than I thought you'd last letting me invade your space. But I'm glad you did."

My usual quiet solitude was made better by her presence. Tally is noisy. As hell. But I love that about her. The only time she's quiet is when she's sleeping and even then she snores.

But hearing her around the house makes it feel like a home. Knowing she's there, even if we're not in the same room is strangely comforting.

The way she sings off key, makes a mess while making the simplest shit in the kitchen and laughs at her own jokes. All of it sounds like home. And I'm not trying to give up my home just yet.

Not that I have a choice. I know she has no obligation to be here.

"So, yea. I'm leaving" She seems hesitant before waving her phone in my general direction. "And I've got a date tonight."

Those six innocent words slice through me, wounding me more than having four teeth extracted with minimal anesthesia. Tally is a grown woman and knows nothing about my feelings for her. She's free to date whoever, but I won't lie like I'm not shocked.

She hasn't talked about dating in forever and the timing feels like a blow to the gut. That's what the fuck I get for holding on to a fantasy that she didn't consent to...

Tally shifts on the cushion beside me, her arm brushing mine and sending my pulse through the stratosphere. Conflicting thoughts of her being this close but planning to go on a date are battling in my dome right now.

"It's been a fucking drought," Tally groans, ignorant to the impact of her words. "If I'm going to fix that I have to stop avoiding dates."

Her voice is resolute. Like it took a lot for her to come to the decision to start dating again.

"Right?"

When she looks at me with a question in her eyes, waiting for me to confirm what she's said, my first instinct is to burst our friendship bubble and confess my feelings.

But I don't do that. She'd be suspicious of the timing anyway. Why the fuck haven't I said anything before now?

"I guess," I push out through tightly clamped lips.

Suddenly hyperaware of the dull ache throbbing in my chest, I chew the inside of my cheek trying to avert my eyes when I see her open a text thread with CeCe to ask for advice about what to wear.

It's none of my fucking business, I try to remind myself.

Needless to say, the half-hearted reminder doesn't help.

This is made even more clear when I realize I'm clenching my teeth and sending unnecessary pain radiating throughout my already sore jaw.

I need to get my shit together.

"To be honest, I'm nervous Pierre. I haven't wanted to fuck anyone in a long time," she says bluntly. Like she always does. Never one to mince words, Tally goes into a rant about being tired of relying on her battery-operated boyfriend.

She spares no details because in her mind she's talking to her very best friend since grade school. And since I'm too pussy to say anything, there's no reason for her to think otherwise at this point.

When my only response is a subtle nod, she gives a huff and carries on.

"Shit, I just hope he's bearable. I get so easily turned off by everyone these days it's starting to make me nervous. I just need one that sticks. You know?"

One that sticks.

The thought alone makes me see red. Tally is not mine. She doesn't **belong** *to me, but the mention of her potentially hooking up with someone who isn't me activates an innate territorial response even I don't expect.*

By the time she leaves two hours later, I'm just about nonverbal. Thankfully, she attributes it to me being tired and tosses me a sunny smile before reminding me that CeCe dropped off soup and there's plenty of ice cream in the freezer.

I spend the next hour trying to convince myself that the chemistry I feel isn't one-sided. But just because there's chemistry does not mean there are feelings attached to it…

A logical person knows that. But am I a logical person?

Hell no. Not when it comes to Tally…

I'm still sitting around feeling sorry for myself thoughts hours later when my phone buzzes with a notification from her.

Open the door, *is all the text says.*

Seconds later I'm pulling open the door to a smiling Tally.

"Miss me?" *she grins, stepping into the house and reclaiming the space she'd only vacated for a few short hours.*

Calm immediately washes over me, eroding the tension embedded deep into every muscle in my body.

"What are you doing here? What happened to your date?"

Tally kisses her teeth and shrugs dramatically. "He got called away for work in the middle of it."

"In the middle of **what** exactly?" *My mind won't even let me consider the fact that they might have been fucking or on their way to that when the date abruptly ended.*

There's laughter in Tally's voice when she responds, but I don't find shit funny. If he touched her... "Dinner, Pierre. He got called away from dinner. Why is your mind in the gutter?"

My head is in a lot of places when it comes to Tally. A lot of fucked up places, to be fucking honest. I have no business entertaining the thoughts I have about her daily. But again, here we are.

And the outfit she has on is not helping.

A short black skirt, a top that's barely there and heels to elevate her short stature. She looks good enough to—

"Fuck!" *she groans.* "I'm starting to think I'm never getting laid at this point."

Her words interrupt my dirty thoughts but send me right into a tailspin of even nastier ones.

Tally. Getting laid.

Not exactly a conversation I was prepared to have for a second time today.

I watch wordlessly as she continues talking but none of the words make it to my ears. All I can focus on is the way her skirt keeps shifting higher and higher the more she waves her arms around, shifting from one foot to another as she tries to convey her message.

"Pierre?"

The sound of my name has my eyes snapping back to her expectant pair. The confused set of her brows lets me know she's confused by my silence.

Without thinking, I blurt the first thing that comes to mind.

"Let it be me."

A frown precedes her next question, "What?"

"The man who ends your drought." I don't know why I'm feeling so bold all of a sudden, but I double down, refusing to break eye contact. "Let it be me."

22.

TALULLA

Present Day

"Do you ever miss my mom?" I ask my dad as he changes lanes on the highway. We're headed north towards the airport an hour away so that I can drop him off and take his truck back home.

He hates paying for airport parking and honestly, I don't blame him. It's not like I have anything else I could be doing at the moment. And I'd gladly drop it all to cater to him anyway.

Frowning, my dad splits a glance between me and the open road, and I can read the discontent all over his handsome face.

"Where is this coming from?"

Being ex-communicated by my best friend because I couldn't keep my legs closed or open my heart, seems a bit dramatic for a casual car talk, so I deflect.

"I don't know, dad. Your life just could have been different is all." I bite my tongue and refrain from revealing everything I know. It's been years since my discovery and we're almost at the airport anyway. There truly isn't enough time for it all.

The way things went left with Pierre has me in my feelings even more than usual. I can't really blame my mother for my inability to trust love completely, but the root of it *did* begin with her.

Thanks to the years of therapy my father paid for from the time I was twelve, I know I have a disorganized attachment style. I crave love in its truest form but at the same time I push it away or self-sabotage until I'm alone.

I am my own worst enemy and the only one standing in my way when it comes to love. But knowing that and doing something about it are two different things. Not to mention, I kind of stopped going to therapy when I got to college. Thought I was all healed up and ready for the world.

The fucking irony. Lucas had served as the perfect reminder that maybe I shouldn't have put myself out there in the first place.

My dad sighs from the driver's seat, the drumming of his fingers against the steering wheel bringing me out of my thoughts and back into the present matter at hand.

"I'm more than okay with my decisions in life, Talulla." His tone is gentle, yet stern enough for me to grasp that he's not here for my skepticism.

"If I had to do it all over again, I'd choose the same outcome. Every time," he says, punctuating his statement.

He's the only person in my life who I've never had to question so I have no trouble making peace with his words.

"Ok, daddy. I believe you."

I catch him watching me from the corner of his and I bite down a smirk. I'd definitely inherited my side-eye from him.

Silence blankets the car as we get closer to our exit and my thoughts start whirling again.

It's not exactly true that my dad is the *only* person who's never made me question them. Pierre falls in that category, too. Everything he's ever said to me from the moment I met him, has been solid gold. Never even a white lie to spare my feelings on occasion. Pierre shoots from the hip no matter what and that's what I love—

"We're not done with this conversation," my dad promises, interrupting a thought that I don't even know if I was prepared to finish.

We pull up to the drop off zone for his terminal and I unbuckle my seatbelt.

Nodding in agreement with he said, I hop down from the truck as he grabs his bags from the back.

We meet on the sidewalk in front of the entrance, and no one shoos us away because this airport is tiny and traffic is all but nonexistent.

My father reaches down to hug me and pulls back with a pensive look on his face.

"You know, you usually drop me off with Pierre and he keeps you company on the drive back. You sure you're ok to head back alone?"

Just hearing Pierre's name has me wincing involuntarily, but I smoothly play it off like I'm squinting from the sun.

"You saying you don't trust me to drive your baby?" I tease, shifting the attention from my lack of a travel companion to his precious Range Rover.

"I trust you with my life, baby girl. But you know that's not why I brought it up."

"Daddy…"

"Fine, avoid me all you want now. But when I get back in town, just know we got words. Something isn't right and I'm going to get to the bottom of it."

"Don't waste your time worrying about me. Go be great on your trip. I love you, daddy."

"I love you more, cupcake."

♥

Isaac's mouth is moving but I honestly don't hear a word.

I've been spaced out for most of the night, replaying what happened in the greenhouse two days ago. Specifically, the final words Pierre uttered to me before he walked out.

Truthfully, I should have canceled this date, but I didn't even remember we'd planned it until an hour before he was set to pick me up.

Typically, I'd gladly welcome any distraction to assist me in forgetting about the intensity of these complicated, conflicting feelings I've been harboring in the aftermath of what went down. But tonight, I can barely focus enough to put one foot in front of the other.

Pierre hasn't answered a single call or text from me in seventy-two hours.

The irony of his silence after I just did the same thing to him is not lost on me. But his silence feels different. He's never iced me out before.

And I can't confidently say I don't deserve it. Maybe it's *exactly* what I deserve. I'm so used to having full access to him at any given moment that his radio silence is unnerving to say the least.

I broke almost all of my rules for Pierre and yet I still insisted on the weird situationship we fell into.

Remorse trickles over me. A feeling I've never faced when it comes to my open dating situation. I'm not in a relationship with any of these men. These are just dates and we both agreed on that. No promises of more, just good vibes and good company.

But Pierre had gotten caught in the crossfire.

Now all I feel is guilt. It's one emotion that's been kicking me in the ass for the past few days.

Even being here with Isaac right now, all I can think is that I should be home figuring out a way to get through to my best friend.

"You ok over there?" Isaac asks as we approach will-call to pick up the tickets his colleague left for him there.

I look up and meet his beautiful eyes, finding concern lurking in the depths.

Guilt twists the knife in my gut even more. Here I am daydreaming about another man when the one in front of me wants to shower me with attention.

"Let's go to the concession stand," I say, deflecting his question. Something Pierre would call me out on, but Isaac just lets it slip under the radar.

I link my arm with his and come to the conclusion that this needs to be last time I see him. It's only fair to both of us.

As Isaac hands me a box of popcorn, I'm lowkey relieved that we are going to see the ballet in a packed theatre. It leaves no obligation to engage in conversation, not that I think my overactive mind would let me anyway.

♥

The universe is fucking hilarious. That's all I can think while Isaac and I stand at my front door after the date.

"Talulla, before you go inside I need to say something."

Fuck. What now?

I want to groan but what I do instead is ask, "What's going on? Is everything okay?"

"I'm not gonna lie, they could be better." He stuffs his hands into his pocket and exhales lowly. "Listen, I really like spending time with you. But you've made it clear that you're not looking for anything serious and well, I am."

Aw, hell.

"If I'm being honest, I'm getting attached to you."

Every muscle in my face tenses.

"Relax," he laughs, reading my expression. "This isn't the part where I ask you to bend the rules and let me make an honest woman out of you. I respect your boundaries and I want you to do what makes you happy, always."

I release the breath I'd been holding since he started talking. Relief isn't the word.

"But I also need to do what makes me happy. And getting attached to a woman who isn't really looking for a commitment doesn't make me happy."

I can see how uncomfortable he is telling me this and I feel like shit for feeling relieved.

"I get what you're saying," I cut in, giving him an out. "It's better to end it now so neither one of us ends up resenting the other."

"Exactly." An invisible weight seems to lift off of his shoulders and he gives me that dimpled smile that could stop hearts. "I can't act like this is easy because I'm really feeling you Tally. But above everything else, I just want you to be happy. And if not settling down makes you happy then I'm with it. Just from a distance. I didn't expect to like you this much, but you're pretty amazing Tally. And I hope you know that."

The last thing I feel is amazing, but I offer a weak smile at his compliment. It's crazy that I'd made the decision to stop seeing him and then this conversation just falls in my lap. I didn't even have to awkwardly bring it up because Isaac did it for me.

"So, this is it?" I ask, watching him closely.

He inclines his head in agreement.

"I'm sorry if you feel like I wasted your time. That was never my intent."

"That's not how I feel, Tally," he reaches up to cup my chin. "The timing is just off. But I know whoever ends up with you is going to be lucky as hell."

I attempt another smile, but I can feel the instant it falls flat.

I miss Pierre.

Focus, Tally.

"You take care of yourself, alright?"

Nodding, I fidget with my keys. "You, too."

One final hug and an awkward wave later, I enter my house and drop my keys on the table near the door.

"I wish the other conversation I need to have would go that smooth."

♥

Splayed across my couch a few hours later, I'm channel surfing when an image on the weather channel grabs my attention, making me almost drop the remote at my side.

"The low-pressure system we were tracking off the Gulf Coast has been upgraded to a hurricane with wind speeds reported at over one hundred-twenty miles per hour—"

The rest of the meteorologist's words are lost on me as panic swirls in the pit of my stomach, mixing with the dread that's been stationed there since my falling out with Pierre. Nothing has felt right in days, why not add a hurricane to the mix?

Because I fucking hate storms, that's why.

My body feels numb as I gingerly place the remote control on the glass top of the coffee table, careful not to drop it and shatter the surface.

One disaster at a time, I think wryly.

Instinctively, I pull my phone into my hands and open up the message thread with Pierre's name at the top.

I don't realize my finger is shaking until I press the picture for his contact and am presented with the option to FaceTime him or voice call him.

Pressing the phone icon, I hold the phone up to my ear, praying for some stroke of luck that he will answer this time.

My prayers swiftly go unanswered.

In fact, instead of ringing, my call goes straight to voicemail. Which means he's either blocked me or his phone is on Airplane mode.

Hoping for the latter, I end the call without leaving a message and swipe back over to our text thread.

My vision blurs with unshed tears as I type out a text, desperate for some form of contact when I know I don't deserve it.

All this is proving is just how dependent I am on him. For every little thing, I go to him for comfort. And now that I'm left standing in the cold, I regret every single time I took his presence for granted.

Resolved to do the work of self-soothing, I reclaim the remote and open up Amazon Prime. If I can't have my comfort human, then I can have my comfort movie.

The opening number of the 1965 version of *The Sound of Music* is playing in no time on my massive TV. Pulling the crocheted throw blanket from its resting place on the arm of the sofa, I snuggle into the plush cushions trying to relax.

I wake up on the couch sometime later, a headache pounding against my forehead and a crick making it impossible for me to fully rotate my neck.

The sun streaming in from the curtains lets me know a new day has arrived.

My first thought is to grab my phone and check my notifications.

The only banners on the screen are from CeCe and my dad.

Nothing from Pierre. Still feeling like a dejected puppy, I stare at the screen for far too long willing a message to appear.

Coming to terms with my insanity, I push myself off the couch and absentmindedly type out a generic message to my dad. He's in Atlanta for a business conference and plans to be there all week, only adding to the cocktail of panic and hopelessness swimming around in my gut.

There's a storm headed my way and I have never felt more unprepared for anything in my life.

23.
Pierre

"PJ, whoever is chirping your line must be important," my dad speaks after watching me hit 'ignore' for the third time in a row.

In lieu of confirming his suspicions or addressing the fact that he just used the word "chirping," I lift the patio chair closest to me and head for the garage.

Storm prep is in full effect, and I'd much rather focus on that than the fact that I'm ignoring Talulla and we haven't spoken since the greenhouse a week ago.

Ignoring her is not a muscle I've ever had to flex so I'm winging this shit. And it's the hardest thing I've ever had to do in my fucking twenty-nine years of life.

Add that to the fact that we were already not speaking before the greenhouse incident, and anyone would understand why every muscle in my body is permanently tense.

I've never been addicted to anything, but I'm pretty sure this is what withdrawal feels like. Especially when your addiction is calling you non-stop making it damn near impossible to hold your ground.

Aggravated, I sigh and pull on the brim of my hat. With the patio furniture moved inside of my parent's garage and the rest of their lawn décor secured there's nothing left for me to throw my energy into in an attempt to forget about the woman who owns every part of me; mind, body and soul.

The very woman I can't bring myself to hate no matter how much she put me and my emotions through the wringer.

Talulla fucking Evans.

Reading the irritation on my face, my dad reappears in front of me and shakes his bald head.

"Have you made up your mind about relocating?" he asks, staring me down.

I almost want to laugh because the solution I thought I'd devised for that was a wash at this point. The reason I wanted to stay in Belle View wasn't even viable anymore.

Maybe it had never been viable in the first place.

I'm not above admitting that my tunnel vision may have bled into delusion at some point.

I don't know. Hell, all I do know is that I miss her.

Call her.

My pride quickly shuts down that thought.

The last words I'd said to her were as final as they come. Even if I hadn't meant them.

Finally, I meet my dad's eyes again. "Can we make it through this storm before you try to ship me off?"

Amused by my deflection, he wavees off my concern about the storm. "You know like I do they always make a fuss about these damn hurricanes, and we barely get a drizzle."

I chuckle, following him into the house through the side entrance.

What he said wasn't exactly true, but I'm going to let him rock on this one. I don't have the energy to point out the glaring fact that this town has weathered at least ten hurricanes in my lifetime alone.

Because if I were to say that out loud, I'd be reminded of exactly what I'm trying to ignore. Why the guilt gnawing at me feels worse.

Talulla has been afraid of storms for as long as I've known her. I can count on one hand how many times I've seen her cry and three of those times were during a storm.

She freaks the fuck out. More than most. But we usually ride out the bad ones together. Something she likes to call "hurricane parties."

Knowing her dad is out of town, the guilt sucking at my conscience won't let up. Knowing she's on her own and probably scared shitless about facing this alone makes regret bubble up in my chest.

What kind of friend am I?

My dad and I make it to the living room and sit on opposite ends of the large sectional. He's saying something about what we'll need to do at work after the storm next week and it's all going in one ear and out the other.

My thoughts are fastened on Tally and whether she's okay.

You'd know if you picked up her fucking calls.

I disregard the nagging voice in my head, determined to maintain my stance. For once. Something I've never been able to do in the past. But after telling her we couldn't be anything anymore, I realize I probably put my foot in my mouth.

Needing something to do besides sit idly on the couch, I make my way to my parents' kitchen dead set on finding something to eat before I dip and go home.

When my mom walks in the door a few minutes later, she finds me at the center island halfway through a sandwich.

"Hey, Peanut." She smiles warmly at me, dropping some bags on the counter.

Realizing she was probably out with other shoppers trying to clear the shelves at the grocery store, I stand up anticipating there being more shit to bring in the house.

"You got more bags?"

My mom's smile falls like she suddenly remembers something and before I know it, Tally is breezing into the kitchen hands full of reusable bags overflowing with groceries.

Stuck in place at her unexpected arrival, my eyes give her a once over before I swing my gaze back in my mother's direction. Her lips are pressed together like she's trying to keep herself from saying something, but her silence has the opposite effect. It bugs me and makes me wonder if she planned this.

"What's she doing here?"

24.
Talulla

What's she doing here?

Embarrassment choked the angry words I wanted to spew at him.

It's the reason I'd simply reigned in my hurt reaction and went back to my car empty-handed. Even though Ms. Gwen and I had just spent hours weaving through crazy shoppers and raiding the shelves of multiple grocery stores to stock up for the storm.

I pull into my parking spot with nothing to show for it aside from hurt feelings and the same fear that's been nagging at me for the past week.

Fear of this storm.

Fear that Pierre was actually serious when he said we couldn't be anything.

Fear because my dad had tried to get an earlier flight and his flight got grounded so now he's stuck in Atlanta.

Just fear.

Heavy, oppressive, unrelenting panic at this point.

It had slowly started ebbing away when Pierre's mom called me and offered to let me stay at their place to ride out the storm.

But now that fear is back in full force, sending a crippling ache all over my body.

Pierre's words had drawn a line in the sand, instantaneously making me feel alienated from the family that had felt like an extension of mine for the past two decades. Four little words and I felt like an outsider all over again.

I guess I can't even be mad. This is what I deserve for fucking up our friendship and agreeing to sleep with him in the first damn place. Thinking with my pussy was a surefire way to fuck things up and here we are.

Could it have happened at a worser time though? I think the fuck not. I'd laugh if I wasn't so damn worried.

This must be what impending doom feels like, I reason as I get out of the car and head for my condo.

The bag I'd packed and planned to use during my stay at the Lancasters is still in my backseat and I see no point of hauling it back into my house right now.

I don't know why it hadn't occurred to me that Pierre would be there today. They are his parents. He has his own house, but of course he'd be near them to prep for a storm. *Of course*, he would.

And of course, he wouldn't want to see me there when he'd made himself crystal clear last week that we were no longer anything.

A fact that I'd been in denial about until about twenty minutes ago. Now I understood the ignored texts, the denied calls, and the radio silence.

That man was serious.

The disgust that'd been present in his eyes at the greenhouse had blossomed into full out hate. That was the only explanation for the dismissive, cold scowl he threw at me today.

At least that's what I tell myself.

Could Pierre *really* hate me?

Could I *blame* him if he did?

I'm not exactly innocent in any of this. Something that I've always been aware of. Just not to the extent that I've become recently.

Tossing my keys on the counter, I slip onto my favorite bar stool at the island and send a weary glance towards my fridge.

My stomach rumbles in protest but I already know there's nothing inside.

Something I had *tried* to remedy when I went shopping earlier today.

That was successful.

My eyes land on the text on my phone screen: *You can stay with me until the storm passes. I have an extra room and I'd feel better knowing you aren't alone.*

The text is innocent enough, but my brain tells me Isaac only sent it out of pity.

When it was forecasted that Hurricane Carol would hit Belle View as a category four storm in the next few days, he'd reached out to make sure I was okay.

I was, in fact, not okay.

Elbows against the cold granite, I cover my face with my hands, contemplating exactly what I'm going to do. Whatever it is, I need to make the decision sooner than later. Lost in thought, I damn near jump out of my skin when I hear a knock at my door.

Pulling my door open, the last face I expect to see staring back at me is Jayce's.

♥

He looks awkward in my kitchen. Aside from the fact that he's never actually set foot in my house, Jayce looks out of place in my modest kitchen for other reasons.

His tailored suit, expensive shoes and towering height clashing against the small, outdated—but charming—appliances I love, stuffed into the tight space.

He's always been someone I limited to the doorstep so I'm trying to take in his presence and figure out what he wants at the same time.

"Sorry," I start. "What exactly are you doing here?"

Jayce's green eyes land on me after their quick assessment of what's visible of my home from the kitchen. Curiosity lingers in his gaze before it gives way to quiet resolve.

"You haven't been answering my calls, Lulu."

"I've been busy with the winery." It's not exactly a lie, but it's not exactly the *truth* either.

The majority of my time in the last week has been spent in an endless pity party. Never mind the small detail that the wounds I was licking were largely self-inflicted.

"I was worried, so I had to make a trip to see that you were okay. Since there's a storm coming."

My jaw drops open and I pick it up off the floor to ask my next question. "You flew into town because I didn't answer my phone?"

"Yea." Jayce frowns looking at me, his tone matter of fact. Almost as if to ask, *why not?*

"Jayce..."

He cuts me off before I can say another word.

"What are your plans for this storm? I can take you back to New York to wait it out. I have to work, but you're welcome to my apartment. There's plenty of space," his words linger as he goes back to surveying my home.

The thought of being shipped off to one of his many properties and being left alone doesn't not sound as appealing as it should. New York is not in the storm's path, and I'd be safe there. But something has me rooted to the spot, fearful of fleeing even though it's exactly what I want.

Pierre in't in New York.

The reality of that comes crashing down on me, swiftly followed by a niggling reminder that I don't even have access to him anymore. So what if he won't be in New York? Maybe that's a good thing.

If I was smart, I'd take him up on his offer, grab my bag from the car and let him drive us to the next city over where his plane is no doubt fueled up and waiting at the private airport.

But if the past two weeks have proved anything to me, it's that I'm not exactly the greatest when it comes to doing things that are in my best interest.

"I think I'm gonna stick it out here, Jayce. But thank you." I try my hardest to suppress the quiver of my lip and the shakiness in my voice. Maybe then he won't see how terrified I am. But not enough to spend some indefinite time confined to the same space as a man I've never done more than kiss on the cheek.

Jayce looks like he wants to question my decision before another knock sounds at my door, startling me all over again.

"Hold that thought," I tell him frowning. Who could be at my door? CeCe is the only other person in this town who would show up unannounced and she's gone to the west coast with Davi. The only reason she agreed to leave me behind is because she thought I'd be staying with the Lancasters.

I can't wait to call and fill her in about that one.

That still doesn't answer who it could be. No one else is bold enough to show up unannounced. But then again, I hadn't been expecting Jayce to pop up on my doorstep either.

Feeling fully unprepared to see whoever's on the other side of my door, I yank it open and audibly groan.

"You've gotta be fucking kidding me."

25.

PIERRE

"Nice to see you too, princess."

She flinches at the pet name and wearily eyes the bags in my hands.

"Pierre--"

She gets interrupted by someone calling out to her.

As soon as I hear "Lulu" I walk past her and into the house uninvited. My only goal is getting to the kitchen.

When I get there, that nigga from the mayor's mansion is standing in the center of the kitchen looking sorely out of place with an arrogant smirk on his face as he registers my unexpected arrival.

A violent shade of crimson clouds my vision and the faint sound of a door closing lets me know Talulla is on my heels.

Dropping the bags on her kitchen counter, I look him up and down, pushing my hands into my pockets to avoid knocking that smirk off his face.

"And you are?" he asks, his arms crossing over his chest as his eyebrow shoots toward his overly gelled hairline.

Scoffing, I open my mouth only for Tally to appear between us looking irritated by the inconvenience.

"Jayce, this is Pierre. Pierre, this is Jayce." She doesn't elaborate on either side of the introduction and avoids making eye contact with me.

Is this the reason she cut things off with me? So she could parade around town with this cocky motherfucker with too much starch in his pants?

"Oh." Jayce sounds amused. "You're the neighbor."

A little thrown that he knows me by name, my eyes find Talulla and catch the frown marring her pretty face. She doesn't speak though. Just stands there looking like she wants this to be over.

"I was just here to pick her up before the storm touches down." He looks over at her with a little too much possession in his eyes and it sends my blood into a simmering boil. "Lulu, why don't you go grab some of your things? The jet is waiting for us and I have to be back in New York for a meeting by four."

Tally staying rooted in place is the only cue I need before I start speaking.

"Nah, she's good. You can leave."

Confusion shows up on his face before he looks at Tally.

"Lulu? What is he saying?"

My stomach turns at that got damn nickname. "Why you looking at her? I know damn well you heard what the fuck I just said."

Jayce laughs like something is funny and Tally starts rubbing her temples.

"Jayce, you should leave." At his wounded expression, she quickly adds. "So you don't miss your meeting. I'll be fine."

"Lulu are you sure? Bec--"

"I'm positive," she cuts him off. "I'll be fine. I promise."

Still looking unconvinced, he splits a glance between the two of us and starts to talk, but Tally shuts it down.

"Let me walk you out," she says, glaring at me as they exit the kitchen and head down the narrow hall towards her front door.

Triumph dances in my heart even though I know I'm about to hear her mouth when she gets back. But at least I'm not the one she's escorting to the door. Not yet at least.

It feels like an hour passes before she reappears in front of me, anger flashing in her tired eyes.

"Pierre, you have a lot of nerve for somebody who basically just dismissed me from your presence an hour ago."

"Tally, I'm sorry. I didn't mean to make it sound like you shouldn't be there. That was fucked up. And I know my family is your family. I was just surprised to see you."

Ignoring me, she walks over to the bags I placed on the counter and starts digging through them. Seconds later, she pulls out a small box I placed there, confusion washing over her face.

Opening the box, she finds the carrot cake cupcake I picked up on my way here as a peace offering.

"You got me a cupcake?" she asks, distractedly. I smile because she's already peeling back the wrapper.

"Tally, did you hear what I said?"

"Unfortunately," she drones, biting the cupcake.

I grin at her dismissive tone. It doesn't matter that it seems like she'd rather do anything but have this conversation. What matters is that she's talking. To me. After what feels like too long.

My heart is on the verge of pounding out of my chest when she looks over at me with frosting smeared on the corner of her mouth. She still looks pissed but the only thought in my head is how fucking sexy she looks.

I resist the urge to immediately walk over and kiss it off of her. Too soon, her tongue darts out and provides the solution.

"Stay with me," I blurt out, clearly allergic to thinking any of my thoughts through today.

Because my eyes never left her face, I catch the jolt of relief relax her features at the offer. Only for it to be concealed seconds later when she carefully trains her features. A veil slips in place, tucking away her emotions.

"Don't do me any favors based on something your mom said. I know Ms. Gwen cussed your ass out which is why I'm not going to bother doing it right now."

I watch her bring the cupcake to her mouth for another bite. "I don't need a pity invite, like I told Jayce I'll be fine. Alone," she adds to punctuate the dismissal in her words.

Hearing his name fall from her lips again annoys the hell out of me.

"Let's be honest, you're only doing this because you showed up and a man was here. Otherwise, I'd still be getting the cold shoulder." Her eyes sweep over me and she gives a small shake of her head, paying more attention to the cupcake in front of her than me.

"Tally," I plead, walking over to her, and lifting a hand to put on her shoulder.

When she ducks out of my reach, my heart drops to my stomach.

This is why I've kept my distance. Because I knew the second I got around her, I would be a helpless fuck, unable to resist her and whatever spell she put on me. Nothing else can explain why I feel so drawn to her when things are obviously so broken between us.

Again, she won't meet my eyes when she speaks. "You can leave, Pierre."

Her words are even icier than the look in her eyes and a smart man would cut his losses and dip. But it's already been established that I am not a smart man. Not when it comes to Tally. And it's cost me too much already.

"No."

"What do you mean 'no'?" she asks, triggering déjà vu. "It wasn't a question."

"You're not staying here by yourself during a damn hurricane, Talulla."

This time she winces at the use of her full name, and I feel triumphant for getting another show of emotion out of her.

"What if I told you I'd rather be alone than to spend it anywhere near you?"

"Then I'd know you were lying through your teeth because you're scared shitless of anything heavier than a sun shower."

Looking slighted at my words, she drops the cupcake wrapper on the island and points a defiant finger at me.

"The last thing I want to do is wait out this storm with you, Pierre."

"Right, that's why you've been blowing up my phone non-stop for the past week. Probably from the second you found out it was headed our way."

It's a petty blow but worth the fire that ignites her brown eyes, thawing the icy coolness from before.

"Fuck you, Pierre."

We stare at each for a few tense minutes before her eyes drop away.

Feeling victorious, I smile at the way she opens her mouth to speak but quickly closes it as defeat softens the hard lines around her mouth.

"Please, Tally. It's what we've always done," I remind her. "Plus, the power lines in my neighborhood are underground and my house is safer than this old ass building you love so much."

She looks irritated by my comment but lets it slide.

"Just come home with me. I'll feel better having you with me." And that's putting it lightly. Even without a natural disaster headed our way, I'd want her in my house. In my life. Every fucking where. All the fucking time. "If you want to leave as soon as it's safe again, I won't stop you."

I expect another feeble attempt at rejection. Even more so because I know I'm lying. I'm not letting her go anywhere.

Instead of turning me down, I witness her shoulders slump as she moves around me, walking towards her bedroom.

"I have to get pillows. The ones at your house suck," she tosses over her shoulder.

For the first time in a week, I relax hearing something she's said.

Call me crazy but being this close to her has lit a fire under me that I almost thought had been dowsed for good. Hearing the catch in her voice, seeing the defiance in her gaze, feeling the warmth of her proximity and the scent of her existence has me feeling invincible.

My fire has been reignited and I'm more determined than ever to figure out the mess we've made.

As she disappears down the hall, I make a silent vow to myself and Tally that whatever needs to be worked out between us will be solved by the time this damn storm passes.

26.

TALULLA

I'm breaking the "No sleepovers" rule by being here. The thought is almost as unwelcome as most of the other events that transpired today.

I haven't said a word to Pierre since we arrived at his house two hours ago.

I've been holed up in his guest bedroom, noise-cancelling headphones planted firmly against my ears as I binge *The Carmichael Show* on my iPad for what feels like the millionth time.

No part of me could have predicted today ending how it did and I'm still not even sure how I ended up in his house when we technically still aren't even on speaking terms.

The weather is relatively calm for now, with the wind picking up here and there. But there's no surge of rain or power outages and I pray to everything mighty that it remains that way.

Momentarily, I'm more worried about the man who is somewhere on the other side of the guest bedroom door.

I can't get over the way he'd let himself into my house and all but told Jayce to get the hell out of dodge.

The display of two male egos at battle had done very little to help the throbbing at my temples. But I will admit, seeing Pierre stand his ground even after ignoring me all week had made me quiver inside. Just a little.

Maybe all hope isn't lost.

I'm not foolish enough to get lost in that thought too long though. He could simply be doing me a favor by letting me stay here and that's how I'll treat it.

A safe place to land during the storm. Offered by an ex-friend.

And an ex-lover, my subconscious reminds me.

Not that I need a reminder. Three weeks of no sex is not enough to ever let me forget the way he owned every inch of my body.

A sudden pressure against my shoulder has me jumping out of my skin for what feels like the one hundredth time that day. I can't take any more fucking surprises.

Snatching my headphones off my head, I glare at his muscular frame hovering over me.

"Jesus, Pierre. You scared me."

"I knocked and called your name five times." The timbre of his voice washes over me, suddenly making me aware of just how long it's been since I've had the pleasure of listening to him on a regular basis.

He looks amused by my alarm, his eyes glinting under the lowlight of the lamp as he watches me scramble into a seated position against the headboard.

I notice the green velvet durag I gave him for Christmas last year tied around his head to protect his waves. My heart leaps at the sight, suddenly feeling sentimental. It's like he's wearing a piece of me even after all our shit.

His eyes bore into mine, refusing to break contact even though he hasn't explained why he's here.

"What did you want?" I finally manage to ask.

Licking his lips, he puts his hands into the pockets of his sweats and regards me for another long moment. It feels like I'm melting under his stare and for the second time in less than two minutes, I question why I'm all of a sudden feeling so shy around him.

It's Pierre, I reason in my head.

Not to be outdone, my heart emphasizes what my head just tried to minimize.

It's Pierre.

"You hungry?"

Opening my mouth to lie, my face heats in embarrassment as my stomach growls right on cue.

Pierre notices and shakes his head. "That cupcake was the only thing you ate today, huh?"

Reminded of his peace offering and our tense moment in the kitchen, I look away from him and turn off my iPad.

"Come on, I made you something."

"Since when do you know how to cook anything more complex than a grilled cheese?" I ask, climbing out of bed and trying to side-step him. Naturally, he makes it impossible, crowding me into the tight space so that I have to brush past him to get to the door.

If Pierre is nothing else, he's crafty.

I don't miss the satisfied light in his eye or the matching smile on his face at our minimal contact.

He's on my heels as I walk towards his kitchen.

"A lot can change in almost a month, Tally," he says reminding me of just how long it's been since we shared space peacefully. Prior to the greenhouse it had been two weeks. Add to it the eight days since then and we were well on our way to a month of no communication.

And I'm responsible for most of that.

The thought alone is devastating.

Needing to lighten the mood, I tease him.

"Boy please, it's been three weeks. Just enough time for me to have my period and start ovulating again. You're telling me you became a culinary genius in that time?"

Pierre's laugh is a deep rumble that blankets me in warm familiarity. I could listen to his laugh all day.

"I never said I was a genius. Just said things could change. Give me some credit."

We've made it to the kitchen now and I notice two plates are on the table in his little breakfast nook.

Raising my eyebrows at the content of the plate, I look over my shoulder and back at him.

"You sure I'm not going to get sick from eating this?"

He looks pained to say his next words. "Fine, my mom made this and I just reheated it."

"Ah, finally, the truth."

I laugh despite myself and the arrested look on Pierre's face would lead anybody watching us to believe he just watched me hang the stars *and* the moon.

Needing a distraction from the gravity of that thought, I ask, "Which one is mine?"

"Whichever one you want, princess." The suggestive undertone of his words has me slipping into the chair closest to me and clamping my thighs together.

Pierre takes his seat across from me and watches me intently as I pick up my fork.

"Why are you staring at me and not eating?"

"I could stare at you all day, princess."

I drop my fork and it clatters against the plate.

Just twelve hours ago he wanted nothing to do with you and then he shows up at your house and sees another man and he's suddenly Mr. Chivalry.

The reminder from my subconscious is petty, but helpful.

"Pierre, you are confusing." I grab my fork again, coaching my fingers to remain wrapped around the gold utensil.

"Can we call a truce?" he asks, ignoring my assessment of him.

Tilting my head, I tug at the locs near the back of my head and ask a question of my own. "Why? So you can go back to hating me once we're not stuck here together?"

A deathly glare takes hold of his features. "Don't joke about that."

"I'm not joking. You clearly hate me and want nothing to do with me." Saying the words out loud makes lead form in my stomach, stealing my appetite and causing tears to spring to my eyes.

I look down at the plate of food in front of me, suddenly fascinated by the mac and cheese. Anything to avoid his burning gaze.

"Talulla, there's no part of me that could ever hate you. It's fucking impossible. And trust me, I've tried. You're branded into every fiber of my being and hating you would mean hating me. That shit ain't happening."

Even though I'm not looking at him, his words still manage to take my breath away. How the fuck am I supposed to keep my guard up when he says shit like that?

Leaning back in my seat, I spare a glance in his direction and notice his light brown eyes trained keenly on me.

"Fine," I shrug, trying to play off how much his words affected me. "A truce."

27.
Pierre

"Here," I say, placing the mug of tea in front of Talulla.

After dinner, I'd been happy as hell when, instead of going back to the guest room, she'd gotten up and walked to the living room. Meaning I got to spend more time with her without her erecting a wall between us.

Seated on the floor in front of my coffee table, she's currently trying to shuffle a deck of cards. And failing almost comically.

Reminded of the time Josh banned her from our card games, I laugh out loud at seemingly nothing. This earns a raised brow from Tally as she picks up the mug and begins blowing on the peppermint tea.

"What are you laughing at?"

"Just remembered something funny," I say, not giving anything away.

She looks disbelieving but says nothing more as an awkward silence befalls us. Not used to being in her presence and not talking nonstop, I scrub my brain for a quick remedy.

"Twenty-one questions."

"What?" Her eyebrow is hiked up again, confusion shining in her eyes.

"I want to talk to you," I admit, unashamed. "And I'm trying to think of the least awkward way to make sure you don't run back in your room and ignore me for the rest of the night."

Snickering, Tally takes the first sip of her tea and places the mug on a coaster.

"Fine, I'll go first."

"Naturally," I concede, slipping onto the floor beside her.

"What's your favorite color?"

I cut my eyes at her and the smile on her face rips my chest open and places my heart right in her palm.

Jesus fuck, she's beautiful.

"Ok, fine. I'll think of another one."

"Take your time," I say, not caring how obvious it is that I don't want our time together to end.

Talulla looks contemplative, her eyes narrowing on my face as her smile turns thoughtful.

"Okay, I got it."

I tilt my head in anticipation.

"Your mom says you might be moving, is that true?" she asks me in an even tone, her face not giving away how she feels about the possibility.

"It was an option," I tell her honestly.

"Was?"

"I decided to stay."

"Why?"

"Guess," I say meeting her eyes straight on.

Blinking, Tally regards me for a long minute before nodding. She fixes her mouth to ask me another question and I don't have the heart to remind her that it's my turn. I'd picked this game to get her talking anyway, so I'm not about to interrupt it.

"Why did you think you were in love with me?"

My eyes widen because I had not been expecting that. And not just because it was only the second question of the game. I just didn't expect her to broach the subject at all. Not after the way things went south the last time we spoke.

It takes me a minute to decide how I want to approach the question. Settling on the straightforward truth, I answer.

"I don't think shit, I *know*."

This may not have been the conversation I expected when I suggested this game but since she wants to go that route, I'll go along for the ride.

Because just as sure as I know my name is Pierre Jerome Lancaster, Jr. I know I love Talulla Evans. I've never been more sure of anything in my life.

"Ok, but *why*?" she asks, staring directly into my eyes.

My immediate instinct is frustration because it feels like a slap in the face for her to question my love. But the fear clearly present in her deep brown orbs stops my retort.

Tally's legs are crossed in front of her. Her hand is busy twisting locs around her finger.

She's *scared*.

This whole time I've been fed up that she couldn't give me what I wanted in return and had never considered she might just be scared.

Fucking terrified, from the look on her face.

"You wanna know why I love you?"

"Yea," she whispers, her hand dropping away from hair as she reaches for the mug of tea again. She doesn't take a sip though, but lets the mug warm her hands as she awaits my response.

I sigh and say the words that have been on the tip of my tongue for ages now. At least that what it feels like.

"You tell anybody who will listen that we're best friends," I start.

"We are." She eyes me wearily and then tries to correct herself. "We were."

Laughing at the absurdity of her statement, I shake my head. "If you think that changed in a week, I got a surprise for you, sweetheart."

She finally moves the cup to her lips, and I smile as she goes back to avoiding my eyes.

"You are my best friend. But more than that, you are my best everything, Talulla." I pause when I hear her gasp but keep talking so I don't lose my nerve. "Your friendship is the best thing that ever happened to me. I love your softness. Man, it's the greatest gift on earth. I love how free you are. I love that you're carefree, but not careless as my mama always says.. I love that you're so warm, Tally. I love that you're super affectionate too."

I laugh recalling how I'd adjusted to her love language: physical touch.

"I don't know how you got me, but now I love that shit. I crave your touch even when you're not around. Not sexually, either." I shake my head, not wanting to minimize the point. "I just want you next to me or near me at any given moment. That's what made the past few weeks the hardest. Not being able to touch you, feel you, smell you. Your absence left a huge hole."

Her eyes widen at my confession.

But I'm not done.

"If we took sex off the table, I'd still choose you. Every time, Tally. Because above everything else, I love doing nothing with you. Eating with you. Vibing with you. I'm better because I know you. I want to make everything easier for you because that's what you do for me, whether you realize it or not. You teach me to slow the fuck down and enjoy the moment in front of me. You're never in a rush and that shit used to irk me, but now I get it. There's no need to rush to the next moment or the next big thing if you're happy in the present.

Everyone deserves a friend like you, but I'm not gonna act like I'm not happy that I'm one of the few people you let get close to you. Your charm attracts a whole lot of attention, but I know you're pickier than you put on. Look at you and all those damn rules," I finish on a dry laugh even though those rules are the bane of my goddamn existence. And the reason we're in this weird ass limbo as it is.

I can't believe I just said all that shit. But every word of it was true. It's gone unspoken for way too long.

"Wow," Tally finally utters after a long moment of silence.

It feels like a weight has been lifted off my chest but placed directly onto her shoulders. I can't explain it, but the feeling is palpable, and I wish I wasn't feeling so relieved while she's clearly panicking.

I try to lighten the mood.

"Remember that time I was getting bullied by Renee in the fifth grade? And you offered to fight her for me?"

"Yea," she nods. "She beat my ass too."

We both bust out in laughter at the memory.

"Why the hell did you offer to fight her for me if you knew you couldn't?" I ask once we calm down enough. My side is hurting from the workout I just got.

"You always looked out for me from the time I moved here, and I wanted to return the favor. You were my only safe place besides my dad, and I wanted to kill that heffa for coming at you."

My heart squeezes at her confession. And the urge to touch her grows even more.

I was her safe place.

"Well, that's when I knew we would be in each other's lives forever," I tell her, my hands itching to run through her locs to massage her scalp. Just because I know it'll have a calming effect on her.

"Can I touch you?" I'm only asking because the thought of her flinching away from my touch again is unbearable.

Tally's eyes find mine. "Is that one of your questions?"

My lips curve upward. "Sure."

"Yes, Pierre." She sighs lightly. "You can touch me."

Like a kid freed in a candy store, my hands race to her neck. With my palm encompassing it, my fingers start kneading at the knots of tension.

Instantly, her head falls back relaxing into the touch. Why had she denied me of this for so long?

The soft rasp of her voice breaks through my rampant thoughts. There's still a hint of laughter in her voice as she continues to travel down memory lane.

"At least by high school I was smart enough to get CeCe on my side. We tag teamed mean-ass Yolanda and she never bothered you again."

I grimace at the memory of my ex-girlfriend from tenth grade. When I broke up with her right before Homecoming week, she'd gone berserk on me, claiming I was robbing her of some rite of passage. *Whatever that meant.*

"Yea, I remember that shit. You and CeCe did a real good job of acting insane. She was terrified," I chuckle as I recall the way they'd stayed up the night before watching wrestling videos.

Not boxing, but wrestling. Don't ask.

Neither one of them had a fighting bone in their bodies. It was the funniest thing I'd ever seen.

"We weren't acting!" she exclaims. "Nobody bothered you or us after that," she states proudly.

I snicker at her, not confirming whether she's right or wrong.

"They knew what the fuck was going on," she goes on.

Hands still busy at her neck, my eyes wander to the photos lined up on my mantle, chronicling the years of our friendship. CeCe's hair goes from purple to lime green to blonde to turquoise. I smile, remembering each phase and shift of our friendship dynamic.

Whether she knows it or not, her question triggered unforgettable memories that have me feeling a way. Long story short, Talulla and Celeste would forever be gold in my book though. Solid gold.

Growing up, it was hard for people to understand how my two best friends were chicks. Especially with how eccentric Tally and CeCe were—*are*. They weren't popular and didn't want to be. And they gave no fucks about what anyone thought. Then there was me. The country-bred, high school athlete and middle child with a chip on my shoulder.

Honestly, it wasn't until college that I even realized my only male friends were my brothers.

Plenty of people assumed I was gay. Others assumed we were in some sort of throuple relationship. Whole time we were just vibing, naturally drawn to each other.

They just happened to be the two people who were always in my corner. Hell or high water. And I'll never forget that.

Things had changed after college though. When Tally returned home after years away. I was shocked to find out the crush I'd developed on her towards the end of high school hadn't gone any-damn-where. If anything, the fascination I'd had with her from childhood had blossomed into full out love.

But she wasn't the same Tally who'd left Belle View six years prior when we were eighteen. She'd gotten her heart broken and she'd built a thick, cement wall around it, blaming herself for someone else's carelessness.

Which is where the rules came in. I know she only made them to protect herself. And they work for her. For the most part. We walked a blurred line where her rules were concerned. Well, we *had* until they won.

Going out on a limb, I swing the conversation back to our "game" that doesn't feel so much like a game anymore.

"Why are you so afraid of my love, Tally?"

28.
TALULLA

I tense under his touch, but don't pull away from him completely. I know he'd just pull me back anyway. And truthfully, his hands feel too good to deprive myself. Especially since he's moved from massaging my neck to my scalp.

"I never said I was scared," I say, finding my voice.

"You don't have to, princess. It's written all over your face. All over your actions."

He's right.

I turn over the words in my brain for a while, trying to decide what I want to say until I land on the truth.

"It's complicated."

His hand stops moving against my scalp, and I know what he's about to say.

"Let me finish."

His fingers start working again as I try to piece together exactly what I want to divulge. More importantly, *how* I want to do it.

"When I was sixteen, I found out my mom tried to come back."

He freezes beside me and this time I know it's out of shock.

I continue while I have the courage to say what I need to say.

"I was snooping in my dad's attic for my Christmas gifts, and I ended up finding a letter instead." I laugh drily although I find nothing about what I'm about to say remotely funny. "She wanted to send me to live with my aunt so her and my dad could be together without the stress of me."

"Shit," I hear at my side, but I don't look over at him, terrified to find pity in his eyes. Something I can't take at the moment.

"Miriam never wanted to be a mother. It didn't matter that I made good grades or stayed out of trouble. Any ounce of responsibility was too much for a burden she never wanted to carry in the first place."

My chest is burning at the memory of my discovery.

"I felt unwanted." I pull my knees to my chest and try not to rock back and forth—a soothing technique I've leaned on for years. "Not to mention embarrassed. Ashamed that my dad wouldn't get his happily ever after with someone who clearly loved him just because of me."

"Tally…"

"No, it's true. If it wasn't for me, they could have been happy together." I drop my chin against my arms folded atop my knees. "He never told me about the letter, and I never told him I saw it."

"Why not?" his voice is calm but full of emotion. One of the dominant emotions being curiosity.

"I know my dad loves me. And I didn't want him to feel worse about the situation." I shake my head, trying to clear the unwanted feelings creeping to the surface. "I spent so much time wishing I had been lovable or just not born. And I promised to never get my hopes up when it came to love. Then I met Lucas and he swept me off my feet. I thought I hit the jackpot. I felt *safe* again. And we know how that story ends."

Again, I laugh without a trace of humor. Pierre doesn't say anything, but I know he's listening intently as I go on.

"It took me years to get over that hurt. He basically confirmed all the beliefs I had built as a result of being abandoned. He did it too, he just veiled it with false promises. Something my mother never bothered to offer. And I felt validated and heartbroken at the same time when the truth came out."

I shake my head and sigh. "He proved that people who say they love me will eventually leave. But I blamed myself a little, too. We dated for years. How could I be that naïve?" I ask no one in particular.

"It wasn't your fault, Tally." Pierre's words are comforting, and I know he means well.

With a sigh, I continue, "So, I promised to never endure that again. Two major heartbreaks were enough to last me a lifetime. I never wanted to let anyone get close enough to leave me again. That's why I created a situation that worked for me. That I could control. Men I could date at arm's length. And it was going great until it wasn't. Until you said you were in love with me. I never planned for that."

Pierre looks at me but doesn't say a word. The beautiful features of his handsome face drawn in concentration. For once, I'm grateful for his silence.

"I thought it would pass and it didn't. So, I knew I had to let you go. Because as much as I wanted to believe you loved me, I didn't know how to love you back. You deserve reciprocity, Pierre. You're one of the sweetest humans I know, and I know you hate that word. But I just want you to love someone who can love you back." I swallow the lump in my throat, willing my voice to stop shaking. "You don't deserve me and my mess."

"You don't get to decide what I deserve, Tally." Pierre's voice is thick, tight with emotion and unspoken words.

"I *know* you don't deserve me," I restate, my words more explosive than I expect. Pierre deserves nothing but kindness, generosity, and unlimited happiness. Not my cagey version of love.

He looks pained at my words and my heart stutters. I'm smacked in the face with the irresistible urge to apologize.

"But I'm sorry something I did hurt you. I was selfish. We never should have crossed that line. But we can't erase what we've done. I just want you to know that I'm sorry. I know this is a long-winded way to answer your question, but you've always called me dramatic for a reason."

I hope to get a laugh out of him, but his face doesn't move. It looks to be set in stone as he absorbs everything I've just said.

Clearing my throat, I finish, "The funniest part is that I did what I did because I am so attached to your family and didn't want to mess it up. But I still did that anyway." My words trail as I remember his claim that we couldn't be anything and my heart breaks all over again.

A thick silence stretches between us, swallowing all of my words and giving nothing in return. I've never said those things to anyone before and the gravity of what I've just done hits me all at once.

The room feels hotter than it did five minutes ago.

Suddenly, I feel clammy and uncomfortable with my proximity to him.

I need air and I need it fast. Setting the mug on the coaster in front of me, I push to my feet and desert Pierre on the living room floor.

"Tally," he calls after me. The bewilderment in his voice is unmistakable.

And I wish I could explain. But I just need a minute. I make it to his back door with choppy breaths leaving my body and pull it open.

The air outside is tranquil, even though I know a storm is barreling towards us and expected to make landfall at some point tomorrow afternoon. There isn't even a breeze as nighttime blankets the quiet suburban neighborhood where I've spent most of my life.

Pulling air into my lungs, I blink into the darkness not really seeing anything.

Instead, I train my attention on what I can hear.

1. Crickets chirping
2. My bare foot tapping anxiously against his deck.
3. Pierre's footsteps drawing closer and closer.

Since I left his backdoor wide open it makes sense that he would eventually come assess what's got me all riled up.

But I don't know if I'm up for talking. Or explaining exactly why I'm having this reaction. Whenever Miriam is mentioned, this involuntary response takes over me and I feel like a passenger in my own body.

"Tally," he says, appearing in the doorway. I don't look up, but I know he's there from the way the light spilling out of the house is abruptly eclipsed by his tall frame.

"I'm fine, Pierre."

"Ok, princess. Whatever you say." He doesn't pry. He doesn't minimize what I've said even though I know he can see that I'm not fine. He's just there. Present.

"I just need a minute." My whisper is strained as I'm still trying to catch my breath from a sudden attack of pure panic.

He doesn't say anything. But he does walk out on to the deck and take a seat directly across from me. I feel his eyes on me even in the dark, an inexplicable calm radiating off of him and seeping under my skin.

One minute turns into five. And five minutes turns into what feels like an hour. Pierre doesn't come any closer, but he doesn't leave me on my own either. He stays right there in his chair watching over me like the angel he is.

Even if he never confessed his love for me, I feel it now just like I always have. His actions shout louder than any words he could ever utter. And that knowledge has something blooming in my heart that I've been trying to deny for months. As soon as I felt the roots latch on to my heart strings, I knew I was in trouble. Because as much as I tried to fight it, I know without a doubt that I love him too. Fully. Completely. And unapologetically. I'm in love with Pierre Lancaster.

My breathing returns to normal, my heart reclaims a healthy cadence and the hefty boulder of tension resting square on my shoulders doesn't seem so heavy anymore.

Finally, I'm able to relish in the stillness of the night, the absent rustling of bushes and the familiar quiet of this neighborhood. I inhale deeply, filling my lungs with air as everything around me gently reminds that this is just the calm before the storm.

♥

29.
PIERRE

Last summer

I pull up the bottom of my shirt to wipe the stinging sweat from my eyes. The Junior League basketball team I coach every weekend had left over an hour ago, but my brother Marcus conned me into a pick-up game shortly after.

The community center gymnasium is almost empty now as most of the other players went home after the last game and I'm walking to the sidelines to get my shit when I see her.

"Ol' girl is here," Marc grunts under his breath, not quiet enough because Tally rolls her pretty brown eyes at him when she hears it.

"Hello to you too, Marcus."

Marcus and Tally exchange pleasantries with each other. They have weird ass banter, but I know he's got a soft spot for her. We've known Tally for damn near twenty years and all other bullshit aside, she's family.

"Talulla, where's mine?" he asks, pointing to the drink in her hand.

"At the smoothie shop," she counters, smiling sweetly.

Marc erupts in laughter, "You ain't shit, sis."

"Love you, too," she calls out to his retreating back.

Marc throws up two fingers letting us know he's leaving, and I focus all of my attention on the woman in front of me.

I take her in. All of her. From the bright red skirt that does nothing to cover her beautiful legs and what looks like a bikini top made from yarn covering the upper part of her petite frame.

Her gorgeous body is on full display, but it wouldn't be Tally if she wasn't showing skin. Her confidence coupled with the fact that she looks good in everything she puts on has always been one of my favorite things about her.

One of the many *things I love about her.*

I'm convinced she could make a trash bag look seductive and I'd walk proudly beside her as she rocked it, too.

"What are you doing here?" I want to know.

"Wanted to see you," she shrugs as I shoulder the gym bag I brought with me earlier.

Her words are simple enough but trigger an avalanche of complicated emotions to come crashing down on me. I don't know why the knowledge that she sought me out "just because" has me feeling like an emotional simp at the moment. We're best friends and see each other just because all the time. Why am I acting like this is some groundbreaking moment?

Tally extends the protein shake in my direction. There is still paper covering half of the straw to let me know she hasn't had any yet. But I know as soon as I take my first sip, she's going to be asking me for some.

Why not just get one for herself? She'd claim she didn't want a full one, just a sip.

"You look good," I compliment after taking my first sip. Just as I suspected, it's my favorite peanut butter whey protein shake from the shop near her house. Despite multiple arguments about the protein and other nutritional content, Tally teases me saying it's just an excuse for me to have a milkshake after I work out.

"Thanks," she purrs, speeding up to walk in front of me in a full out strut. "One of CeCe's new sets and I had to have it," she twirls with a smile on her face that robs me of my ability to think straight.

She looks radiant. Like a spotlight is shining just for her in some far-off corner and hitting her at the perfect angle.

For once I don't find fault with the onlookers as we walk through the lobby. Talulla knows how to steal the show without trying. Her effortless charm is what draws most people in, me included.

But beyond the charm, there's warmth and depth that not many people get to see. I'm one of the lucky few and I don't take that shit for granted.

Outside, I place my hand at the small of her back to move her towards the inside of the road, placing my body between her and the light flow of traffic in our suburban neighborhood.

As we switch places, her nose wrinkles after her elbow comes in contact with my sweaty shirt.

"Pierre, you need a shower."

I throw my head back, cracking up at her audacity.

"Yea aight, Tally. Don't forget I know what you smell like after a few hours of flag football or skating," I remind her jokingly.

It's her turn to laugh as we start the twenty-minute walk.

The sign for the neighborhood where we grew up, Belle Heights, slowly comes into view. The neighborhood came about in the '70s. When the Black middle class in Belle View was finally earning enough to be able to invest in real estate.

The neighborhood has stayed over ninety-five percent Black since it started. Most of the houses had been built in the '70s and '80s but renovated over the years. The house I bought a year ago was a new construction and sits on land near the back of the neighborhood.

I live one block over from her dad's house and I figure that's where she's left her car because the only thing she was holding inside was the shake.

"Yea, you got me there," she concedes, a light giggle lilting her words.

I love her laugh.

You love everything about her, *a voice in my head taunts as we continue walking.*

Again, I'm reminded of how the mundane feels like everything whenever she's around. From the corner of my eye, I study her face in the low glow of the streetlights stunned as always by her effortless beauty.

"Here," I say extending the cup in her direction.

She looks relieved that I finally offered her some and takes a big ass sip.

Shaking my head, my only thought is how much I love the way I feel when I'm around her.

It's easy yet stimulating. Calming yet exciting. When I try to put it into words, it doesn't make much sense. Hell, I'd be better off naming the feeling after her. Since she's the only person who's ever evoked the twin sense of serenity and quiet urgency deep inside of me.

I may not be able to adequately express it, but something as simple as walking home together while we share a protein shake makes me feel like the luckiest man alive.

I grab her hand with my free one, bringing her fingers to my lips. Brushing a kiss against the center of her palm, I watch the tender smile claim her face.

"What's that about?" she asks, quirking her brow at me.

"I don't need a reason to kiss on you."

Her teeth make an appearance as she bites down on her bottom lip, golden-hued eyes lingering on me.

"What are you doing tonight?"

She looks over to me awaiting my answer as we start walking again.

"It's spades night," *I tell her.* My brothers, Josh, Marcus, and our dad and uncles get together a couple times a month to play the game that Tally claims she can't grasp for the life of her.

"Ah," *she shakes her head.* "I would invite myself to crash but Josh banned me after last time." *She puts her hands at her sides and there's a petulant frown on her pretty face. I can't hold in my laughter.*

She'd really pissed Josh off the last time he'd taken her under his wing and tried to teach her. By the end of that night, he'd jokingly banned her from any spades games in the future but she was taking that shit to heart.

"You can still come." Matter of fact, I want her there now that the thought has been thrown out there.

"It's okay," Tally says politely turning me down. "My dad and I are going out tonight before he leaves town anyway. But I hope y'all have fun. I'll stop by if it's not too late when I get back."

She'd snuffed my hope and reignited it in the same breath.

"It won't be too late. Even if I'm sleeping, just call me and I'll get up for you."

Tally stops walking and looks at me. I'm distracted by the image she creates in front of me. Like fucking artwork. The dusky backdrop makes her look like a painting.

"Talulla in Red," I muse to myself giving the imaginary painting a title. I'll have to send CeCe a personal thank you text for designing this get up. It looked like it was literally made for Talulla and no one else. No one else could rock it the way she is.

It looks like she wants to say something but decides on "Okay" just as we reach her father's driveway.

When I turn to continue my short walk home, all I can think about is the possibility of seeing her again tonight and that shit has me lowkey hype.

30.

Pierre

Present Day

Dreaming about Talulla seems like adequate punishment for letting her go to bed last night without correcting every incorrect thing she'd said.

Every belief about her being unlovable and not being capable of love had punched me directly in the chest until pain was shooting through every part of me.

But words had failed me, and I didn't want to say the wrong thing. Not when she'd looked so terrified sitting on my back porch. Like she regretted opening up to me when all I could do was rejoice that she trusted me enough to say anything in the first place. No matter how painful it must have been for her.

So, when she'd walked back into the house and headed straight for the guest bedroom, shutting the door softly I let her, not wanting to push her past her limit.

I pull myself out of bed, still stuck on the dream about last summer. It was right after we'd started fucking. As a way to "end her drought." Before I'd ever confessed any feelings besides sexual ones for her. Still, I'm surprised that Tally couldn't tell I was head over heels for her on that walk home.

I feel like it'd been radiating off of me.

After washing my face and brushing my teeth, I open my bedroom door and step into the hall. Seeing the door still closed at the opposite end of the hall, I feel comforted by the fact that maybe she's getting some rest.

That thought goes out the window when I round the corner and find Tally sitting in my favorite spot on the couch. One knee is pulled to her chest and her hair is brushing her shoulders as she stares down at her phone, oblivious to my arrival.

Remembering how scared she got yesterday when I "snuck up" on her, I clear my throat and wait for her to acknowledge me.

"Hey." Tired eyes look up at me. The rasp in her voice is evidence that she didn't sleep well or that she spent part of her night crying behind closed doors. Maybe both. And that possibility fucks me up.

Needing to be in her orbit, I abandon my plans of going to the kitchen and join her on the couch. The scent of her welcomes me as she tosses her phone aside, abandoning the weather update I know she was reading.

"Did you sleep ok?"

A half-hearted shrug precedes her answer before she clucks her tongue. "I haven't slept in days."

Furrowing my brow at her statement, I stare at her long and hard. I know if I ask why, I'm going to be partially implicated in her answer. Even if she doesn't outright say it.

"Tell me how to fix it."

"What?"

She sounds lost and for good reason. I've made a habit out of blurting things out lately. The filter between my brain and my mouth is broken.

"This. *Us*. I'll do anything."

I want to absorb the pain I heard in her voice last night. Hell, I'd strap it to my back and walk a thousand miles with it weighing me down if it means relief for her.

If I could, it would already be done. And I'd carry it all with a smile on my face if it meant she never had to feel that way again. But that's not the case. And without a way to remedy it, I'm feeling lost on what I *can* do.

It's the first time she's been that real with me. Which is strange to say since we've been friends for so many years.

My arm finds a resting place against the back cushion of the couch and to my relief, Tally inches closer to me.

"There's nothing to fix," she tells me, melting against my side and initiating the most contact we've had in weeks. I grin, resting my chin on top of her head as my arm wraps around her snugly. More than happy that her need for affection won out over the distance that's been lingering between us for weeks now.

Even while I relish the feel of her softness against me, her words trigger a memory of me and Marcus in my mom's kitchen. Him telling me the same thing. That I couldn't fix everything and that maybe I should be there in the way she needs me.

"Things just are what they are. But you being here is enough for me. You seeing me and really hearing me." She pauses to look at me directly. "It's everything."

More peace than I've felt in a long time settles over me with her assuring words.

"But I have a request," Tally slips in just as I'm starting to relax.

"Whatever you want is yours, Tally."

Softness overpowers every other emotion on her face as she looks up at me with a gentle smile before telling me about this request.

"Let's promise to never give each other the silent treatment again. No matter what. I should have never done it and it's a really fucked up way to "handle" things," she says, framing her words with air quotes. "I don't want us to do it anymore."

"Ok," I say easily. Ignoring her had been the hardest thing I ever did in my life. I'd gladly take a vow to never do it again. It goes against everything I believe in anyway. There's never a day that I don't want her to have access to me.

"Promise me."

When I look down, her coffee-colored eyes are burning into the side of my face, expectantly waiting for my confirmation.

"Cross my heart." I take it one step further. "If something is wrong, we fix it by talking it out. No running away. If we need space, cool. But no icing each other out."

She looks completely relieved at that, nodding her head as she shifts her weight against me on the couch.

"Good," she sighs and it's barely a whisper.

If I wasn't so tuned in to her, I would have missed it.

"I'm used to losing people, Pierre. But not you. It can never be you. I'll go insane. I was well on my way before we squashed this yesterday," she laughs lightly and my heart twists. "You've been in my life longer than my mom was. Longer than Lucas. Longer than anyone besides my dad and I can't lose that. I *won't* lose that." It sounds like she wants to say more but stops herself.

Greedily, I wonder what she's leaving unsaid, but realize she's already said a damn mouthful. I let every single word sink in and kiss her temple.

"You're never going to lose me, Tally."

♥

When she told me she needed a distraction from the storm, I didn't expect this.

Didn't expect her to fall to her knees after lunch and start showing me how much she *missed* me.

Her tongue is hugging my dick, her cheeks hollowed out as she moves her head back and forth to push me further and further down her throat.

Any remaining common sense I had, left the instant she kneeled before me with that cunning smile on her face and her hand snaking up my leg.

Fuck, she owns me.

Every part of me.

There is no one on this earth who makes me feel this good. This tortured. This fucking alive.

"Shit... fuck," I groan, unable to stop the words.

She's gagging, her eyes glossy with tears as she looks up at me refusing to break eye contact as I come undone. My hips jerk on their own accord and my fist captures a handful of locs as I ride the wave.

One of her hands is secured around the shaft of my dick and the other one is massaging my balls. This alone has me fucking harder into her mouth, hitting the back of her throat over and over again.

Feeling the vibrations of her moan on my length as she stares up at me with shining eyes tips me over the edge.

My dick swells, making her mouth even tighter around me as I come in her mouth, shooting hot spurts of my seed straight down her throat.

"Shit, Tally," I swear, trying to catch my breath as I pull myself free from her mouth with an audible *'pop.'* "I wasn't expecting that."

She looks triumphant as she watches me fight to catch my breath. Her mouth is still partially open as she stares up at me. Hypnotized, I watch as she licks her lips and swallows. Knowing that the rest of my seed just went down her throat has me hard again in seconds.

I need to be inside of her.

"Stand up," I growl.

31.
TALULLA

The thrill that shoots through me at being tossed on the bed is a welcome feeling.

My body sinks against the softness of his mattress as Pierre places a knee between my legs and joins me on the bed. Hovering over me, his eyes are dark and frenzied.

Staring up at him, my breath leaves my body in shallow puffs as everything on my body begins to throb sinfully.

Jesus, this man is fine.

Revenge is written all over his face and I can't wait for whatever he's about to do to me.

The heat emitting from his body is enough to make me overheat with anticipation. I want him. Everywhere. In my mouth again. In my hand. In my pussy.

I want it all. And I wish he'd stop prolonging it.

He hasn't touched me since he put me on the bed. My clothes are still intact. Between the two of us, the only thing exposed is his dick which is growing harder by the minute, despite the deposit he just shot down my throat less than five minutes ago.

"Pierre," I groan, and I don't care that I'm whining. The only thing I know is that I want him, and he seems intent on staring a hole into my soul.

"What princess, what do you want?"

"I want you but you're not doing anything," I state plainly, frowning at the satisfied smile on his face.

"You want me?"

My frown deepens and I push up on my elbows to study him. "Are you just going to echo everything I say?"

Again, his smirk returns, and his tongue bathes his lips as he stares down at me with something mischievous simmering in his eyes.

Finally, Pierre inches closer to me and his hand falls against my legs, his coarse fingertips tracing up my thighs until he reaches the hem of my shorts.

"You're waiting for me to do something?" he asks, and the gravelly tone of his voice has me melting deeper into the mattress.

"Yea." It's the only thing I manage to say as he slips his hand up further, brushing against the crotch of my shorts.

The simple movement has me gasping for air.

"Why are you waiting, princess?" Pierre asks, his fingers moving lazily but deliberately against the thin sliver of material sheathing my pussy.

"Pierre."

His hand comes to a halt near my entrance.

"Why are you waiting, princess?" he asks again, he eyes boring into mine as he waits for my response. A response I don't feel capable of giving.

Gulping, I try to shift my hips in a way that will bring his fingers back into contact with my pulsing center.

"Pierre, baby please…"

He snatches his hand away altogether and his smirk turns into a full out grin.

"I love it when you call me baby. You haven't done it a while."

Sucking in air, I reach out to grab his arm, but he skillfully avoids my grip. The revenge in his eyes earlier suddenly makes sense.

"Pierre, I'll call you whatever you want if you just come back to me."

"You need to learn to trust me, princess."

Confusion breaks through my lusty haze as I stare up at him.

"What are you talking about? I do trust you."

"No." Pierre shakes his head, "You don't."

"Yes, I do--"

"If you trusted me," Pierre starts as his hand finds the seat of my shorts. I can feel the wetness soaking the material when he presses down, and it only turns me on more. "You'd know I'd never hurt you. Intentionally or otherwise."

Moaning, my eyes roll back as he moves my shorts aside and slips his index finger up and down my slit. The wetness leaking out of my core makes it even more exhilarating. My whole body twitches in anticipation for what's next.

"If you trusted me," Pierre starts again, his eyes latching on to mine and refusing to look away. "You'd let me make my own decisions about the type of love I deserve. You'd let me show you that I have no interest in repeating the fucked-up cycles you've experienced before."

I hear his words, but truthfully, they aren't sinking in.

His finger moves up and swirls around the tight bud of my clit, drawing a strangled cry out of my throat.

It feels so good, and I'm immediately lost in the sensation, lifting my pelvis up to meet him so that I never have to go without feeling it. Not even for a second.

"Pierre, that feels so good…" my words trail as my legs fall open even more, giving him full access to have his way with me.

The rough pad of his finger moves against my clit rhythmically, pulling me closer to orgasm with each passing second. Pleasure is building at the base of my tummy, threatening to explode and fan outward. And all I want is the touch that's going to push me over the edge.

Hips undulating against his hand, my hand covers his as he continues to work me into a frenzy.

I'm so close.

Suddenly, my center is bare again. The absence of his hand has me feeling bereft and annoyed.

"Pierre!"

"You want to come?"

I don't justify that with an answer. My scowl does all the talking.

Hypnotized, I watch him lift his hand to his mouth and lick all traces of me off his finger.

"You taste so good, princess."

"Pierre." There's an edginess in my voice as my desire mixes with annoyance.

"I need you to understand something before I let you come."

"What?" I snap.

My tone pulls a rumbling laugh from him.

"I love you, Talulla."

My petulance falls away. I want to tell him I love him, too but the words clog in my throat, not yet confident enough to be said aloud. But I know I do. I feel it, too.

"And I need you to trust me. I can make decisions for myself, princess. You don't get to tell me what kind of love I do and don't deserve."

"But—"

"And you don't get to sit around and take the blame for other people's fucked up actions. You're not unlovable. You're not wrong for loving them and getting hurt. That's on them. They're fucked up and if it was possible, I'd hunt them both down personally and beat their asses because they broke someone I love more than anything. Someone I'd give the world to. Someone who doesn't believe she deserves it because of their actions."

"Pierre."

He moves over me at the sound of his name, supporting himself on his hands as he cages me between his arms and the bed.

Showering kisses over my face, he stops to press his forehead against mine.

"I love you, Talulla. And if you let me, I'll prove it to you."

I can't believe he's doing this to me. Right now. Like this.

"Do you hear me?"

I nod, unable to form words at the moment.

"You understand that I love you and that I'm not going anywhere--

I feel like crying. God, I hope I'm not crying.

"Tally?" he says, expectantly.

"I hear you, Pierre.

Searching my face, he looks satisfied with what he sees because he lifts up and starts pulling my clothes off of me unceremoniously.

Because I was only wearing the shorts and a bandeau top, it happens quickly.

Wonder fills his eyes as he looks over me, fully exposed to him. There's only a tiny splinter of lust in his gaze, it's overridden by open adoration and amazement.

"I missed you so much," he whispers and the hoarseness in his voice sends butterflies dancing in my stomach.

"I missed you too," I confess, my eyes glued to him as he continues to watch me.

A ravenous glint takes over his expression at my words and he pulls his own shirt over his head. In seconds, he's back between my legs positioning the tip of his dick at my eager entrance.

"I'm never going to stop loving you," Pierre declares before pushing into me and stealing any chance of a response from my lips with a scorching kiss.

Caught off guard the sudden fullness of his intrusion, I scream his name as my back arches off of the bed trying to create more room for him.

My wetness welcomes him, and I wrap my legs around his waist pulling him closer to me. The pleasure of his nearness overrides every ounce of discomfort from being stretched to the limit. I want him as deep as he can go.

He feels too good, and it's been too long since we've done this.

My heart is strumming uncontrollably in my chest.

"Don't ever run from me again, princess." He slams into me again and the stroke reverberates straight through to my soul, pulsating outward until it consumes all of me.

I swear I can feel him in my chest, branding my heart with each thrust.

"I'm fucking serious. You are mine." He growls out the words as his pelvis falls against mine creating a friction that has my head spinning in the fucking clouds.

A moan is all I can muster up under his assault.

"This is what you wanted, right?"

I don't even know my name right now. Let alone an answer to his question. But internally, I agree.

Yes, this is exactly what I wanted. What I've always wanted. What I'll always want.

"You're mine and I'm never letting you go."

All I hear after that is a whimper and I suddenly realize that it was me who made the sound.

"Give me your hands." Our fingers lock as he continues to steadily rock into me, stretching me out and maintaining eye contact that has my eyes watering. His gaze is so intense it makes me uneasy. I feel like I can see his soul bared to me. "Don't let me go, princess."

"I won't."

"You promise?" He wants to know, nipping at my bottom lip with his teeth before kissing the pain away.

My toes curl into the sheets, but I remember he's expecting an answer.

"Cross my heart."

32.
TALULLA

By the time Hurricane Carol blew into Belle View, she'd lost a lot of steam and had been downgraded to a category two storm. Because the storm had slowed down so much, it took her all her afternoon and late into the evening to do her thing before it calmed down outside.

Pierre, thoughtful man that he is, gave me my noise cancelling earphones and ate me until I was literally too delirious to focus on anything other than relearning how to breathe properly.

Luckily, we never loss power and I was able to further distract myself by cooking us dinner.

After eating, I picked up the phone I hadn't touched all day and found texts from CeCe, my dad, Isaac, and Jayce.

My eyes nearly crossed from the multiple notifications, but I opened the message thread I thought would be easiest to navigate first.

Isaac: *Just checking on you. Text me to let me know you're good, T.*

Isaac: *It's been a minute. You good? I'm not trying to bother you, but I'm starting to worry.*

The messages had been delivered six hours apart. And the latest one was almost two hours ago.

Shit.

Typing out a quick response, I let him know I'm perfectly safe and thank him for the check-in.

Moving on to Jayce's thread, I roll my eyes at his dramatics. Because he is who he is, he'd sent a long string of one-sentence texts instead of confining them to one or two lengthy messages.

Jayce: *Lulu, I'm disappointed.*

Jayce: *Are you seriously ignoring me for that gardener?*

Jayce: *You told me he was your neighbor and childhood friend*

Jayce: *When did that change and how you could you possibly choose him over me?*

I stop reading after the fourth one and blow out a loud sigh. In two simple steps, he's blocked. I know I could have made time to have a conversation with him. I know what I just did is avoidant and petty. I know all of that. But we're taking baby steps over here and he was getting on my damn nerves.

"You good?" Pierre asks, walking back into the kitchen after being holed up in his office to do some work for a while.

He looks at me with nothing but bad intentions painted all over his face and I instinctively start backing up.

"Pierre, I'm already sore. Stop," I giggle.

"What?" He feigns innocence. "I was just trying to make sure you're good."

His smirk says otherwise, and I grin looking back down at my phone. "Yea, right."

Coming up behind me, he plants a kiss on my neck and wraps his arms around my waist.

"Thank you for dinner. It was amazing," he says into my hair.

"You already thanked me," I say reminding him.

"I know, but I'm still thinking about it. I wish you cooked more often. You're good at it."

Smiling fondly, I sway with him as he rocks us from side to side.

"Pierre, to let you tell it I'm good at everything." The man is my biggest cheerleader.

Laughing, he pulls away from me slightly and corrects my statement. "Everything except fighting, princess."

Instantly, I crack up because I knew he was going to say that shit.

"But other than that, yea I'll ride for you."

Tickled by his vote of confidence, I catch his gaze and turn in his arms.

"Pierre, do you really think I used you for sex?"

He jerks his head back and his forehead crinkles from the frown blanketing his handsome face.

"Damn Tally, where did that come from?" Confusion is cloaking his usually confident tone.

"You said it," I remind him. "In the greenhouse. It was one of the last things you said to me."

Sighing heavily, Pierre drops his playful demeanor.

"I thought we already established that everything I said that day was bullshit. I never thought you were using me and I never actually wanted to stop seeing you, Tally."

"You know I care about you. Right?"

He looks lost on why I'm saying this, so I clarify.

"I just want you to know that. If you ever feel like I'm using you, in any way, I hope you'll tell me and not wait for it to become an actual problem."

"What if I want you to use me?" he asks, his brow lifting as he regards me.

Snickering, I shake my head and cross my arms at my chest.

"I want to tell you something," I reveal, watching his face carefully.

"What's up?"

"You know how you always told me that I would be good working with kids?"

He nods instantly because it's something he's told me any time I'll listen.

"Well, last month I took your advice and applied for something at the children's library."

"And?" he asks, expectantly.

"I got it, I've been volunteering as the guest storyteller for a little over a month now and I really like it," I say, squeezing my eyes shut.

I know he's going to be happy for me, but I still brace myself for his reaction because I waited so long to tell.

Disbelief, shock and pride flash across his face before he gives me the warmest smile I've gotten from him in a long time.

"For real?"

"Yea."

"What? Why didn't you tell me sooner?" His hands are at my shoulders, running up and down my arms as if he can't contain his excitement.

It's fucking adorable. I love that he can be this happy for me about a volunteer position.

"I wanted to make sure I was actually good at it before I told you and got embarrassed," I say truthfully.

"What? Of course, you're good at it. You're Talulla Fucking Evans. You're a natural when it comes to kids. Everybody loves you, Tally."

"Well, last week they told me about a different position that opened up. A paying position as the assistant coordinator for the children's program. I don't have a degree in Library Science or Education so I can only apply for the assistant position. But I think I'd be a good fit. It's only four days a week and my time would still mostly be mine. Plus, the kids who go there are so damn cute," I gush and finally take a pause.

When I see the look on Pierre's face, he's glowing with pride. But love is also shining in his eyes. Something that seems to be the norm for him since I got to his house the other day.

I have never met a man who wears his heart directly on his sleeve the way that he does. It still manages to catch me off guard.

"You're incredible, Tally. If you really want that position, I know it's already yours. They'd be crazy not to hire you."

"You think so?" I ask, suddenly timid.

"I know so. I'm so damn proud of you, princess."

I love this man.

And I'm so close to blurting it out that I question myself on why I don't. I tell myself that I just need more time. Just a little more time and I'll tell him.

33.

PIERRE

Waking up beside Talulla has got to beat any other moment in my life by a long shot.

Last night was the first time we slept in the same bed together. Exhausted from the rounds we did, Tally had patiently waited for me to change the sheets before climbing back into bed to sleep with me last night.

In the moment, it had felt like a victory but actually waking up to see her still there makes me feel like I won the lottery.

Talulla "No Sleepovers" Evans finally caved and broke her rule. For me.

Yea, I'm fucking excited.

Even more so because she's somehow wrapped herself around me like a tangled headphone cord, her legs entwined with mine as her head rests on my shoulder right under my chin.

She's lying more on me than the bed.

I've never been more comfortable with being uncomfortable in my life. The pressure of her weight against me calmed me into a deep sleep all night, both of us sleeping straight through the last of the storm.

Tally shifts against me, mumbling something as she drags her hand from my chest down to my waist and squeezes tight. She doesn't wake up fully, the action seeming to be enough to lull her back to sleep.

I know at some point I need to get up and check around the house outside for damage. I need to check if there is any power and call my parents. All of those things are important, but right now all that exists is this.

All I want is this.

♥

"Pierre, I think I'm in love with you," Tally blurts out across from at the dinner table.

A neutral expression is cloaking her face as she stares back at me.

She said it like she was reporting the news. And that's the part that has me stuck.

Because across the table from her, my heart slams to a stop.

"What?" All other words escape me as I try to process the words she's just said.

The breath is knocked out of me and suddenly, I don't know what the hell to do with my hands or my eyes.

"Sorry," she looks embarrassed. "I don't know why I said it like that."

This is real?

She opens her mouth to speak again and all I can do is stare at her, transfixed.

"I don't know where it came from." She shrugs, sipping her wine.

I bet my mouth is hanging open right now and I don't even care.

"Well, I *know*," she corrects herself. "It seemed so obvious, and I probably have been for a while. But I finally admitted it to myself and now I'm telling you."

She gives me an unsure smile and waits for me to say something.

"Tally…" I don't recognize my own voice when I hear it. I sound strangled and fucking desperate. "Don't play with me."

Tilting her head to the side, she frowns at me. A dip forms between her brows and she bites her lip in contemplation.

"What do you mean? Why would I be playing with you?"

Yea, why *would* she do that?

"I told CeCe and she wasn't surprised." She grumbles, still speaking as if she's sharing info with an old friend she hasn't seen in a while. Not like someone who just confessed their love for me over dinner.

What the fuck?

I try to get a firm grip on reality and hope my voice sounds less manic when I ask, "What do you mean you told CeCe you're in love with me?"

"The other night," Tally supplies, "On FaceTime." She looks confused by my question, like what she's saying is the most obvious thing in the world. "After I told you what happened with my mom and I went back to the guest room."

Am I dreaming?

What the hell is happening right now?

I grip the handle of my fork with too much force, needing something to anchor me to reality.

"So, you're saying you're in love with me?" I ask again, just to be sure.

This is new territory. And I don't know how to fucking act.

For so long, my love has existed as a one-sided pipe dream, unrequited but definitely there. No matter what. There's never even been a hint that it would ever be returned, and I was coming to terms with that. Knowing that I would always love her, and she would give me what she could until that changed. It had finally started being enough for me.

Now *this*.

Shit.

She's in love with me.

Fuck.

It's what I wanted for so long and now that it's in my lap, I don't even have the words.

"Yes. Pierre, I'm in love with you."

With my gaze riveted to her face, I watch the emotion pass over her features as she says the words aloud again. It's the same expression that

I've seen there for the last couple of months and could never put a name to it.

And now I know it's love.

"I love you," she sighs. "That part I've always known. It's pretty hard not to love someone who has been in my life as long as you have. But I didn't know I was *in love* with you until a month or two ago. I just hadn't admitted it to myself yet, so it was hard for me to put a name to it. I didn't even realize I *could* be in love again."

Her eyes find mine and the smile I love so much is covering her face.

"But I did eventually figure it out. When you were the first person I wanted to call about anything. When you would look at me and all I felt was peace. When being around you was better than any other crazy thing I could be doing at the moment. When you're the only man I've felt comfortable having sex with in years. When I sat back and thought about all that, that's when I knew," she says with a nod. "Yea, I should have known."

"Tally."

"I should have figured it out a long time ago, but I was in denial. And scared like you said. But I do love you, Pierre. I love you so much."

Before she finishes that statement, I'm around the table and lifting her out of her chair. Holding her body tight against me, my lips crash into hers robbing her of the chance to continue talking.

I kiss her hard, with every bottled-up emotion and unspoken word I've never gotten to share with her. I throw it all into the kiss and calm settles into my veins as she lets me kiss her. Really kiss her.

Something I've never had the privilege of doing outside the bedroom.

Her lips welcome mine, kissing me back as she wraps her arms around my neck.

"You love me?" I ask, biting down on her bottom lip softly, trying to give us both a break to catch our breath.

"Yes, I love you."

"You mean it?"

"With all my heart," she answers easily, and it has me dropping my forehead against hers.

"I love you too, Tally."

"I know," she laughs, breathily. Then she pecks my lips and stares up at me. "Now what?"

Because Marcus had primed me for this question, my answer comes easily.

"Now, I ask you on a date."

Her eyebrows lift in question.

"A real date. I'm not letting you keep me in the house like your damn sneaky link anymore."

Tally pouts. "You don't like being my sneaky link?"

I know she's teasing me. The love in her eyes is clear as day as she stares up at me and I don't think there will ever be a feeling that tops this. No fucking way.

"Just answer this question, Tally. Will you go on a date with me?"

"Yes."

34.

Talulla

My feet carry me over the grounds of Talulla Manor as I inspect the damage from the storm. It's been a week since Hurricane Carol swept through Belle View and the surrounding areas. And I've finally made my way to the manor to see what the pictures my staff sent me couldn't show me.

Aside from a few downed trees and a brief power outage, no significant damage had been done. But, until things are back to a hundred percent, we'll be closed to tours and overnight guests.

"Penny for your thoughts, cupcake," my dad prompts from beside me.

He's finally back in town and volunteered to come with me to survey the damage. Thankfully, there isn't much for us to "fix" aside from landscaping issues.

"I'm grateful, that's all."

"Because there's no damage?"

"That, among other things."

My dad cuts his eyes at me suspiciously. "Would one of these other things happen to be that I left town and came back a week later to you being in a relationship with Pierre?"

Giggling, I shake my head. "We're taking it day by day."

There is still a mountain of things I need to unpack in therapy before I hitch my wagon to anyone. Even if that someone is as understanding as Pierre.

We both agreed to take it as slow as we need in order to build a healthy foundation. It doesn't change our actions toward each other, we just aren't rushing to pin a label on it.

Pierre says as long as he finally has me, *exclusively*, he couldn't give a fuck about what we're calling it. And I have to agree.

My dad clearly has other thoughts in his head.

"Whatever you say, cupcake. But I've seen the way that boy looks at you. And I've seen the way you've been looking at him lately. There's a whole lot of forever in those glances."

Slipping my arm through his, I search his face and see an overflowing amount of pride.

"As long as you're happy, cupcake. That's all I care about."

"I am happy, dad." I couldn't say that I had ever been *unhappy*, but I had been in search of something. Something I had finally found. It'd gotten messy. And heartbreaking at times but at least no one could take it away from me.

"That's what I like to hear."

"What about you, Dad? Are you happy?"

My dad pauses to think about my question, and I wish I had the ability to read minds so that I could see what he's filtering out.

"I'm getting there, cupcake," he finally says.

His answer is more candid than I expected. I thought he'd just brush me off with an "of course" and keep it pushing.

But the rawness I hear in his voice intrigues me.

"You remember that question you asked me last week? About me missing your mom?"

Involuntarily, I still at the mention of Miriam and wait for his next words.

"I do miss her."

I know I'd been the one to ask but his answer feels like a slap in the face. It's not his fault at all but I'm still too stunned to speak.

She had been his wife. They had taken vows together. It makes sense that he misses her. I just wasn't expecting to hear him actually admit it.

"I miss the version of her that I married," he clarifies as my thoughts run rampant. "By the time she disappeared, she wasn't that woman anymore."

Oh.

"So, to answer your question, I don't miss the woman who left. I miss the woman I married, and I miss the idea of the life that I thought we would have together."

"Oh, dad," my voice cracks as my heart breaks for him all over again.

"Let me be clear though. I don't miss the woman who abandoned you…us. I don't know that woman. I figured out too late that I'd fallen in love with an illusion. And any woman who could turn their back on an innocent child—especially one as brilliant as you—was not a woman worth my love. We decided to have you…together. And then she started to resent me for trapping her when we'd made the decision together. By the time she finally left, I wasn't really surprised but I was still devastated. I never wanted you to experience that, cupcake. But it would have been worse if she stayed. I will admit that I spent most of the time after she left focused on creating a "normal" life for you. Well, as normal as I could as a single parent."

"You did an amazing job." And I mean every word.

"Thanks, cupcake." He leans down to plant a kiss at my temple. "I did the best I could. It wasn't until recently that I realized I haven't really processed anything. I pushed all the resentment and hurt down because I didn't want you to be affected. But now that you've been out of the house for a while, I realized that I was still stuck emotionally on that day she left. Twenty years have passed but I haven't moved past it. Not emotionally…" His words trail.

Silence falls between us as his confession sinks in.

I look just like my mom. It must have sucked having a living reminder of his greatest loss running around the house every day.

When I look up, I realize we've reached the courtyard. Minimal debris covers the cobblestone as we walk over to a bench near the center.

"I never knew you were still holding onto that," I say quietly.

"I don't even think I knew." He shakes his head beside me. "Not until recently."

My heart aches for him, and not just because he's my dad. If I'd heard his story from a stranger, I'd still be heartbroken.

Curiosity gets the best of me. "What's helping you process it?"

My dad chuckles drily. "Talk therapy, friends and finding new hobbies that don't revolve around suppressing how I really feel. The jury is still out on what's the most effective, but I'm starting to feel better and that's gotta count for something."

"That counts for everything," I say soothingly as I rest my head on his shoulder. "I'm proud of you, dad."

"Not as proud as I am of you, cupcake."

♥

"Based on what you're telling me, you have it in your mind that everyone you love will leave. Does that sound correct?"

I nod feebly at my therapist as she eyes me with her astute eyes.

"It's a perfectly normal reaction to have when someone has experienced the kind of loss that you have."

Whew!

Why did it make me feel better that other people felt just as fucked up as I did? I'm sure that's a question I can ask her in a future session. It just feels good knowing I'm not alone in this. That my heart isn't the only one both yearning and pushing away love.

"In instances like this, I've found that it can be helpful to have a list of exceptions ready whenever those intrusive thoughts try to get to you. Why don't we take some time now and come up with a list?"

Seconds later, she's staring at me curiously.

"Your dad, Celeste, Ms. Gwen," she repeats back to me.

I nod.

"Why didn't you say Pierre?" she asks, her gaze locked on me.

I'd done it purposefully, but now that she'd pointed it out, my heart sank. Why *couldn't* I see him in that light?

"I don't know."

"He's been your friend since grade school, correct?"

"Right?"

"Has he ever done anything to make you think he would just up and leave?"

"No."

"But he still wasn't on the list…interesting."

"I love him," I blurt out, feeling the need to save face.

"You love him, but you don't trust that he won't leave you?"

The sigh I let out is heavy and repentant.

"Let's unpack that."

Pierre's Epilogue

Six months later.

"We need to get you a new car," I tell Tally as I walk through the door of her condo.

I'd just gotten back from my cousin's shop after getting her car worked on and my legs were cramped like a bitch from sitting in that tiny ass coupe.

"There's nothing wrong with my car," she claims as she walks in the room.

As always, a smile I can't control takes over when I see her. Half of her locs are up while the rest fall around her shoulders. She has on denim overalls with only a sports bra underneath and she's barefoot as she closes the distance between us.

"Someone got a haircut," she notes, before going on tiptoes to greet me with a kiss.

Six months in and I'm still gassed every time she kisses me. That shit might seem small to some people but being able to just kiss her whenever I feel like it is something that I'll drink to on any day.

Tally reaches up to wipe her gloss off of my lips after the kiss and smiles.

"Guess what?"

"What's up, princess?"

"I finished the first draft of my book today!"

She jumps up and down, pulling a laugh from me. I love how excited she gets. That shit is adorable.

"Congratulations, baby." Easily, I pull her back into my arms and wrap her in my embrace.

A few months ago, Tally decided she wanted to try her hand at writing a children's book. As her personal hype man, I fully supported that idea and had been there every step of the way while she figured out the story she wanted to tell.

When she decided on a backyard full of talking plants trying to recover after a bad storm, I couldn't do anything but cheer her on. Her creativity didn't surprise me, but it was still fascinating to watch in action. Teaching kids how to bounce back after an unexpected challenge through talking plants was fucking brilliant.

"I got you something," I tell her. I'd planned to give it to her just because but now that she has good news it's even better.

Looking around, she sees nothing out of the ordinary in her living room and raises her brow. "What is it?"

"Hold up," I tell her, walking back to the front of her condo. Opening the door, I find the plant that I left there five minutes ago and pick it up.

I barely make it in the door before Tally is screaming like she won the damn jackpot.

"Oh my god!"

The Philodendron Pink Princess. Rare as fuck. Just like Tally.

"Pierre! I only mentioned that I wanted this once. Like months ago."

"I know," I smirk as she hugs the pot of the plant close to her like it's a human. This woman…

The first time she brought it up, we were watching a TV show. The next day I'd gone to work and called every supplier trying to find this damn plant. It hadn't been easy, but I was finally able to find a nursery owner willing to cut a piece from one of his plants and let me propagate it at home.

The smile on her face right now is all the validation I need to know that the effort had been worth it.

Part of growing into this relationship with Tally in the last six months has been realizing my lane when it comes to her. Tally was used to getting gifts. That shit was easy to do. But I got off on finding the rare things that she never expected to materialize and then just giving it to her like it was nothing.

Her reactions would never get old.

"Take a picture of me. I wanna show CeCe," Tally demands, shoving her phone towards me.

I capture a few pics of her cheesing before she walks off to find a spot for it in her living room.

"Ooh, maybe it'll be better in my room," she mumbles, disappearing down the hall.

With her distracted, I AirDrop the pictures to myself. One of them will end up being my new screensaver. How the fuck did she make overalls look sexy?

"Where do you want to eat?" I ask, taking my brush out of my pocket. I'd tried a new barber today and I felt like he'd fucked up my wave pattern. I run the brush over my waves and then my beard a few times.

That's how she finds me when she makes it back to the front of her apartment.

Tally looks me up and down and I return the favor. She smirks at me mimicking her actions.

"We had dinner plans?" she asks, biting her lip and I know exactly where he mind is.

"We didn't, but now we have something to celebrate."

"What if we just order in?" she asks, trying to brush up against me.

I sidestep her, shaking my head.

"Nope, I'm not letting you hide me in the house."

"I'm not hiding you!" Tally's laugh echoes around the apartment. "Stop saying that shit."

Still brushing my waves, I grin at her. "I'll take care of my pussy later. Right now I need to make sure you eat so you have energy for what we do later."

253

Suddenly, she ain't got shit to say.

"That sound good to you, princess?"

All I get back is a nod before she goes to find her shoes.

Talulla's Epilogue

One Year Later

"Pierre, I don't think this is working."

Pierre looks up from his laptop just as I snap mine shut.

Writer's block is kicking my ass. After publishing my first book earlier this year, I'd immediately been contacted to write another. I'd finally carved out a day to just write and now the words just weren't flowing.

Pierre's eyes turn sympathetic before he mirrors my actions and closes his laptop.

"What's wrong?" he asks patiently, already standing up to join me at my desk.

"I don't know what to write. Everything I type is trash."

"We both know that's a lie."

"That's what it feels like," I groan, covering my face.

"You wanna take a walk?"

My ears perk up. "Yes!"

I swear, Pierre always knows the exact remedy to whatever problem I'm having. He does it so effortlessly, I sometimes forget how much effort it takes to make it look that way. How deep he has to know me. How deep he has to *love* me to have a list ready to go at any second.

Outside, he grabs my hand as he falls in stride beside me, adjusting his stride to my shorter gait.

Again, I take a minute to appreciate how easily he molds to my wants and needs. And he's never heavy handed with it, it's just second nature at this point and I *still* can't get over it.

There is nothing I won't do for this man because I know, without a doubt, that he would weather any storm just to see me smiling.

I'm so damn happy I finally opened my eyes and saw what was right in front of me.

"Have I ever told you how much of a great provider you are?"

Pierre smirks. "Not today."

"I love everything about the way that you provide for me, baby."

His grip on my hand tightens at my praise.

"I mean it, Pierre. You provide peace, comfort, and protection without blinking an eye. I love you so much. I'm so lucky," my words trail as tears sting my nose.

"Tally, I know your ass ain't crying again."

"I can't help it!" I cry out, rubbing the protruding belly in front of me. These damn hormone surges are straight from the pits of hell, hand delivered by Satan himself.

I hate crying. But so far today I'd cried at breakfast, twice while we were out shopping earlier and now this. It's the most I've cried my whole life. Absolute insanity.

"Come here." Pierre pulls me into his arms and rocks us back and forth, right there on the street.

"Why are you crying?"

"Because I love you," I sniff.

"You sure that's it?" he asks, searching my face.

Nodding, I take comfort in the safety of his embrace before I reluctantly continue walking beside him.

"I love you too, princess," he says belatedly. "Always have, always will. And it's only going to keep getting deeper. You're bringing a life into this world that's an extension of the both of us. I'll never be able to explain to you how that makes me feel."

"Are you sure you aren't mad at me for making you a baby daddy before a husband?"

Pierre snickers, watching me from the corner of his eye. "You say that shit like I didn't have a choice."

I purse my lips.

"I told you that title shit don't bother me. With or without a ring, I already know who I belong to and vice versa. If we ever wanna change that, the courthouse is ten minutes away."

"As long as you're sure...."

"Tally, I've been sure about you for years now. I've just waiting for you to catch up."

Printed in Great Britain
by Amazon